SHE HIDES FOREVER

AN ARTEMIS BLYTHE MYSTERY THRILLER BOOK 2

GEORGIA WAGNER

Contents

PROLOGUE:

ALONE, ROBIN JOGGED ALONG the path, arms pumping, a glaze of sweat now stippling her skin. The white earbuds pulsed with high-tempo music, coaxing her through the woods. Just another step. Just another. Another. She inhaled the scent of lake water, which lingered on the air. The autumn wind carried speckles of chill moisture over the placid, glassy surface. Across the water, she spotted a red kayak scything through the liquid like a swan. The kayak shifted slightly, and for a brief moment, it almost looked as if it were heading towards her.

She shook her head, refocusing on the task at hand. Eyes on the trail, mind on the rhythm of the music, feet thumping against the ground.

The very early morning sunshine only just now peaked over the horizon, but Robin always enjoyed an early start. Her breath came in pants. Her legs pumping as she kept to the trail. The high school track and field meet had been postponed until the weekend, and seeing as this was her last year in school, she wanted to make sure she had a good showing.

There were whispers of a college scholarship in her future. She smiled at the thought, resisting the urge to hum along with the music in her ears.

This portion of the lake trail was segmented by lengths of trodden ground and the occasional overgrowth. Now, her feet found a carpet of moss and grass.

As the song faded, and before the next one could start, she heard, muffled, the faint swish of water lapping the lake shore. This sound was soon accompanied by a faint *splash*. She frowned, glancing off.

The kayak had come to shore.

The bright red vessel had furrowed through the mud, cutting into the ground. But there was no sign of the kayaker.

She hesitated, slowing now, stepping over a fallen branch. Her eyes lifted from the trail, fixating on the abandoned kayak. She could have sworn she had seen someone in the vessel. But now, it sat empty.

She frowned, hesitant. Her mind cast back to the previous week. A woman had drowned in this same lake. In fact, rumors circulated that a few women had recently been killed in Pinelake. This thought sent goosebumps shivering up her arms. She wet her lips, breathing heavily but reaching up shaking fingers to slowly remove an earbud. Now, as the second song started, it only played in one ear. She was no longer moving.

Having come to a complete halt in the middle of the road, she stared towards the lake and the abandoned kayak.

"Hello?" she said, her voice tentative.

No answer. She stared across the water, taking a step towards the small boat. Had the kayaker fallen out? Were they in trouble? She felt a pang of concern replacing her fear. She took a couple of stumbling steps towards the edge of the trail, her breath coming in quick gasps.

She tried to steady herself.

She had grown up in Pinelake. Her father, in fact, was a police sergeant. Her grandfather, a sheriff. Her oldest brother was on the force, along with her middle brother. She hated the place. But she knew she could never tell the others in her family.

Sometimes, it felt as if they were more concerned with keeping outsiders away than they were with helping the people who needed it.

She forced back her fear, stumbling now as she nearly tripped over the discarded branch. She nudged it aside with the tip of one shoe, the sweat along her arms going chill.

She approached the edge of the lake and the abandoned kayak.

There was no movement in the water. No splashing. Only the faintest flutter of ripples across the glassy surface in the wake of the vessel indicating where it had cut through the water to approach the shore.

"Hello?" she said again, louder, her voice creaking.

But still no response. Maybe she had been seeing things. Maybe no one had been in the kayak. There was a paddle stowed just within.

Suddenly she heard a *snap*.

She turned sharply, glancing through the woods. Another loud *crack*.

Movement.

She frowned, feeling the shivers return, her hand tight against her music player. Her father had insisted she carry pepper spray, but she had left it back in the parking lot, in her car.

And then, she went stiff. A doe was crossing the path, fifty yards away. The beautiful deer stared at her, wide, dark eyes blinking beneath the final veil of night. Morning rushed in, and with it, the light ushered the doe scampering into the woods once more.

Robin gave a little laugh of relief.

She turned slowly back, shaking her head, and giving a final glance across the lake. Someone must have left their kayak tied to one of the docks with a bad knot. It must've slipped free. That was the only explanation—

The kayak suddenly moved. Jostled sharply. She let out a squeak of fright as the red boat toppled on its side.

And then, she realized the source of the disturbance. At first, she thought, in horror, that it was an alligator. But there were no alligators in Pinelake.

Not an alligator. A man. An enormous, impossibly large man. He had been beneath the boat, and now he surged up, gasping like some ghoul rising from a grave and drawing air for the first time. The man stared at her with blazing eyes. Briefly, she thought she might recognize him.

She let out a faint protest. He was stumbling towards her now, dripping wet, his clothing plastered to him. Though, there wasn't much clothing at all. His shirt was missing. In fact, he wasn't wearing pants either, or shoes. He had something of a towel wrapped around his waist, pouring lake water which also drenched his skin.

She took a stumbling step back, yelping as she nearly tripped over a branch.

The large man standing on the shore, exhaled, inhaled, and said, quietly, "Three minutes. I held my breath for three minutes."

She was scared again. Her hand was scrambling for her phone. She was now trying to stumble back while also feeling jolts of concern. Was he okay? What was he saying?

He looked at her. "I was given three minutes," he said simply. "So I will give you the same."

She stared at him.

He raised a large hand, flicking his fingers. "You better run now."

The way he said it, the inflection of his tone sent shivers up her spine. She stared at the man, eyes wide. He glared, frowning. "Robin Dawkins," he said firmly, "I know who your family is." His face slick, water on his eyelashes, it was creating a sort of warping effect to her perception of his features. Why did she recognize him?

He pointed a finger at her. "Run," he said quietly. Then louder, "*Run*! You better run!"

He was grinning now, wide, his skin stretched at the lips.

He had been hiding beneath the kayak. Holding his breath. Why? And then her fight or flight kicked in. She yelled, turned on her heel and began to sprint, racing in the other direction.

She thought she heard splashing. Then laughter. "Two minutes left," he yelled. "Only two!"

By the sound of things, he was running through the woods next to her. Chasing her. His large silhouette cut through the undergrowth.

Full terror filled her. She was trying to navigate her phone. At the same time, she was sprinting with all her might. He kept running after her, calling out. "Not long left. Not much longer at all. We're getting near a minute. Just a minute."

He was breathing heavily now and went quiet a few seconds later, racing through the woods behind her, occasionally making a sound or snapping through branches and brambles.

She continued along the trail, desperate, sheer horror prickling her spine. And yet, she was so very far from the parking lot.

So very far from anything.

She tried to scream, but her voice was lost on the wind, beneath the mountains, above the lake.

It was all so beautiful.

A very scenic place to die.

1

Artemis walked through the cold, gray halls, feeling like a rat trapped in a maze. Ahead of her, the prison guard strolled casually forward, whistling, keys jangling at his belt, his night stick swaying with each step. A deep sense of foreboding fell over her like a knitted quilt.

Thick, oppressive and insulating her body from the chill halls. She felt warm. She swallowed, her throat parched. She reached up and brushed her dark hair from her face and cast a glance into the glass at her side. Bulletproof, leading into the visitor's area.

The place had been cleared, of course.

The visit had been scheduled a week before—a favor from Agent Forester for helping them catch a serial killer in Pinelake.

Now, as she glanced through the glass, she caught a faint glimpse of two eyes.

One the color of hazel gold, the other like a sapphire under the moon. Her brother Tommy had the same, different colored eyes but switched.

She looked away. Some called her pretty, but she went out of her way to diminish these accusations. No makeup, only soap instead of perfume, her hair always pulled back in a simple ponytail. She wore plain clothing and no earrings or jewelry.

"Fifteen minutes," the guard reminded her, pausing now in front of a sealed glass and metal door. He stepped back, waiting a moment and waving towards a camera above the door. The hall was lined with cameras, blinking red lights like oracles.

And then, the door buzzed—a loud, jarring screech.

The guard pushed open the door and gestured for Artemis to enter.

She swallowed the lump in her throat. Wishing now, perhaps, she'd taken Tommy's advice. He'd warned her against speaking with their father. Warned her that nothing good would come of it. His exact words had been: *He's a liar. He doesn't know how to tell the truth. Come on, Art—be reasonable.*

He'd also added a few more colorful words towards the end while describing exactly what he thought of their father...

But Artemis *had* to know.

Helen isn't dead...

The message the Ghostkiller had given to Erik Kramer, which he'd conveyed right before trying to stab Artemis. She let out a faint huff of air, shivering where she stood and biting her lip. Was it really worth the conversation?

Fifteen years, she'd managed to avoid her father. Fifteen years she'd been out from under his thumb. And now... here she was, willingly wandering back into the spider's web.

She let out a faint sigh of frustration, biting her lower lip as she so often did when she was nervous. She murmured beneath her breath. *"Knight F3. B6. Knight C3. Bishop B7..."* The memory trick helped soothe her. This time, she was reciting the opening to the very first game she'd ever played in a tournament. She'd lost that particular game.

It was rare, nowadays, for Artemis to lose. Now ranked in the top 80 grandmasters in the world, she was the first woman to break into the prestigious ranks. Some, after her win in Seattle the previous week, were starting to whisper about a potential female victor of the national tournament next month. In the open bracket, this had never been done before either.

But Artemis focused on the game she was now playing in her memory once more. A loss. She could lose. Her father was a genius, too. In fact, her father had been a genius far longer. She swallowed, biting her lip. On a one-off deal, she'd helped the FBI on a case, partly because of her connection to Pinelake but also because of her father's meddling.

He wanted her back in his web. Why? She couldn't say.

But she knew he was enjoying this.

It was often difficult to navigate what a psychopath wanted.

"Arrived!" a voice suddenly crackled from the shoulder microphone of the guard who'd escorted her. Artemis heard another buzz, this time from inside the room. She watched as a brown, metal door slowly opened. She heard jangling, the sound of chains and muttering.

The guard shot her a look. It wasn't quite dispassionate; it even contained a few notes of empathy. "They'll be a minute," the guard said quietly, nodding.

Artemis winced, still biting her lip. She wanted to step through the door, but her body refused the motion. She let out a faint huff of frustration.

Come on, she thought to herself. *Like a band-aid. Get it over with.*

"He won't be able to hurt you," the guard added, clearly noticing her discomfort. "Two guards are with him, and I'll be right here. You'll be fine." He nodded encouragingly.

Artemis felt a flicker of gratitude at his kindness. Out of a desire to reciprocate, she blurted out. "Good luck at the wedding."

He nodded, smiling. "Thank—"

Then he stopped, frowning, likely realizing he hadn't mentioned anything about a wedding. Artemis grimaced. She often kept her observations to herself. But in addition to playing chess through her childhood—though only joining tournaments in her twenties—she'd also been raised by a mentalist. Her father was a charlatan, of course. She didn't believe there were such things as psychics. But he'd taught his daughters and his son—when Tommy was willing to sit still and listen—how to *read* other people. To study their body language, their unspoken words. To watch them closely and only respond to non-verbal cues. A lot could be understood by paying attention to details.

"Did—did I..." the guard began.

But Artemis didn't want to explain herself. She could have pointed out the combination of an overly neat haircut and the faint fragrance of too-strong aftershave suggested an upcoming celebration. The way he'd been tapping his foot nervously near the entrance to the prison while calming as he went deeper suggested something was on his mind, and it wasn't work. His friendly demeanor and chipper attitude suggested it wasn't a funeral nor some distant obligation. Process of elimination left her with only a few celebratory functions.

It was the whistling that cinched the deal. *Ave Maria.* A classical song played at weddings everywhere. It wasn't a *sure* guess. But certainly close enough. And now, judging by his look of awe and surprise, she'd been right. Cold-reading wasn't about *knowing.* It was about fishing confidently. If right, then pretending as if she'd known all along. If wrong, brushing it off as something trivial. Her father had been a master of this.

Not that she cared to make an impression on the guard. She'd only been attempting to be nice in return.

Now, as he stammered after her, she finally found the resolve needed and stepped foot into the air-conditioned visitor's room.

A thick, red line across the threshold indicated where prisoners had to stop. Red paint on the floor provided either instructions or markers to keep prisoners separate from each other and their visitors. There was a very large digital clock behind a white cage, padlocked on the wall above the door. And far more cameras here than had been in the hall.

Again, she felt like a rat in a cage.

She moved between the tables, slowly, approaching the large, bullet-proof glass wall at the far side of the visitor's room. More laminated instructions were taped to the glass, along the frame, providing further directions. She read these quickly—though she'd never been as much of a speed-reader as Helen had been.

The jangling sound from behind the just-open, brown door continued. Then she heard the noises stop. The sound of footsteps. She approached the glass tentatively but refused to sit at first, staring through the translucent surface towards the open, brown door.

And then...

A guard entered first, glanced towards Artemis and indicated one of the plastic seats bolted to the floor on the other side. He leaned forward, clicked a button, and his voice echoed over a speaker built into the wooden counter. "Seat yourself."

She slowly lowered to the cushioned seat, biting her lip again and playing out the final moves of the game she'd lost. She'd sacrificed too many pieces. Had tried to trade material for some type of strategic advantage.

Too aggressive. That was what the Washingtons—her analysts—had told her. Artemis had been too aggressive.

Now she didn't feel aggressive at all. More like a cornered rabbit. She perched on the edge of the cushioned seat, staring through the glass.

And then, following the guard's path—and responding to a gesture of the man's fingers—a new figure entered the room.

She stared, watching as Otto Blythe arrived.

He wore a blue prison uniform with his name and prisoner number stenciled on the lapels. His hair was combed neatly, a bit longer than might normally have been allowed in a prison, but her father had a way of getting things he wanted.

And Otto, above all, cared about appearances.

It was credit to the silver-haired man that as he emerged, he made a prison jumpsuit look more like a lawyer's outfit. Something about the way the collar was turned, the way his shoulders were thrown back—his healthy, energetic stride, as if indifferent to the situation he found himself in.

He smiled politely at the guard indicating the seat and even reached out, his fingers grazing the guard's elbow. "Thank you, Max," her father said.

His voice carried the same, humorous, lilting tone she remembered. A charming voice. A voice always on the verge of laughter. His eyes twinkled in good humor as he nodded graciously at the guard, as if he were some wealthy customer at a hotel tipping a busboy, rather than a prisoner receiving barked directions.

As his fingers grazed Max's elbow, though, the guard shoved him. "Do not *touch* the guards!" Max said. But his heart wasn't in it. If anything, he sounded tired as if he'd issued this instruction before. Like Tommy, Otto wasn't the best at following directions.

And like always, as he stumbled back, holding up his hands in a gesture of apology, his eyes were still twinkling with mirth, his lips still creased in a smile.

The second guard followed into the room, and the brown, metal door shut with a faint, electronic *buzz*.

And then, slowly, her father lowered into a seat.

He looked up, meeting her gaze.

Their eyes met.

His were both hazel, his traditionally handsome features more worn and wrinkled than she remembered them. But not *much* more. When she'd last seen him, his hair had been mostly auburn. Now, though, he was crowned in pure silver. No tattoos, no piercings. Even with slightly curling hair which tumbled past his ears, her father didn't have a strand out of place. His jumper was pristine, well kept, folded at the collar. His hands, in cuffs, were secured to a metal bar on the other side of the glass.

He muttered faint instructions like, "To the left. No—no, another inch. Yes, good job. Thank you."

The guard with the keys locked the bar in place and retreated, leaning against the wall, and staring towards Artemis now.

Her father sat upright, flanked on either side by two security officers. But it almost felt as if he were a CEO in a boardroom, backed by two of his own lackeys.

As he watched her, Artemis' skin crawled.

She stared back at him, refusing to look away. She'd long rehearsed this moment. Often wondered what she might say... And now, sitting there, facing *him,* her tongue was tied. The presence Otto carried was palpable. She remembered, in her mind's eye, the way her king had toppled as she'd surrendered that match from her first tournament.

She shivered at the memory of defeat. Those last few moves...

She'd known she was losing. But had played anyway.

"Hello, dearest," her father said in a slow, velvety voice. The voice of a stage practitioner. The voice of someone accustomed to their own charm. "It's been some time, hasn't it?" He leaned forward, peering through the glass, smiling congenially. "Don't worry, I'm not upset. I'm glad you came."

Her brow flickered into a frown. *Not upset. Glad...* He was already posturing. Teasing, playing with her emotions. With Otto Blythe, one had to listen to what *he* didn't say more than what he did.

"Otto," she said simply.

His expression twisted. A genuine look of pain. Hurt in his eyes, his lower lip quivered, but he bit back a sob and leaned in his chair. "Otto? Artemis—I'm your father. Call me dad—"

"Oh, cut it out," she snapped.

"Cut out what?" he said, his voice shaking on cue.

"You sent Kramer to kill me," she said, her voice like iron. She didn't *want* to look at her father but also refused to give him the satisfaction of looking away.

He pressed fingers to his chest, leaning back in his chair now. Like a snake shedding scales, the emotions vanished from his face. It happened so suddenly that someone unfamiliar with Otto might have been surprised.

But she knew her father's tricks. Knew the games he played.

"I did no such thing," he murmured.

"Why?" she pressed. "Why now?"

He shook his head. "Artemis, listen to me," he said, his voice firm, urgent. He exhaled slowly. "I swear to you. On my soul. On my mother's grave. On my children's lives—I didn't do this! I haven't killed anyone. This is a set-up. I know you don't believe me. But please... please, I'm begging you. If you have *any* kindness in your soul, listen to me. I'm innocent. Art, listen—I *am* innocent!"

She wanted to leave then and there. The worst part of it all—she could *feel* her heart rising in compassion. Could feel her emotions responding while her mind rebelled against his words. "Be quiet," she said softly, staring at her hands now. They were shaking where they pressed to the smooth surface of the counter.

"Ten minutes remaining," snapped the guard, Max, behind the glass.

"Art," her father said, his voice rising, "whoever kidnapped your sister—whoever kidnapped Helen—that's the killer. The *real* killer. You have to believe me. Please."

Artemis said, her voice cold. "And do *not* call me that." She had come here to confirm her father's claims about Helen. Alive... kidnapped by someone else?

And yet she couldn't trust anything her father said… But she needed to know what *he* wanted. Speaking wasn't going to work. She had to do something bold—take something away he wanted.

The only thing she could think of taking away… was herself.

So she pushed up, turning to leave, prickles all along her spine.

2

"Please," he mewled, a pathetic, shaking voice now. He slipped from one emotion to the next, trying them on like outfits, discarding them like obsolete fashion.

Her hands were shaking so badly, she clenched them in front of her, hiding them with her body.

She scowled as she began to march away.

"Fine, fine—whatevs, baby girl. Don't be cold. Come on, let's chat." Another switch to his voice. Disdainful, indifferent, callous. She turned back. He was no longer leaning forward but had reclined, slouching in his seat, the faint curl of silver hair arching over his brow but then brushed nonchalantly to the side.

She frowned at him from halfway across the room. She'd managed to stir *something...* But what was this? So she redirected, forcing the topic *she* wanted to discuss. "You said Helen was alive. I know you're lying."

He looked back at her and then winked. "If you knew that, dear," he said slowly, "You wouldn't have come. How's chess been, by the way? I hear you're winning more games."

She stiffened, swallowing. She hated the idea that her father was able to keep tabs on her even behind bars.

"I hear you live in Salinas now," he said conversationally. "I have some friends down that way. Good friends." He watched her, nodding slowly. "Maybe they could stop by, pay you a visit?" His voice was congenial, playful. The threat was in the eyes, though.

At least, she thought it was. But it was so difficult to tell.

"Maybe they could convince you of my innocence," he said. "It isn't right... You letting me rot in here, Art. It isn't right." He shook his head side to side.

"You killed those women," Artemis murmured. "You strangled them and disposed of them around the mountains, like trash. And you think to lecture me on what is right?"

"I didn't kill *anyone,*" he retorted.

"Mr. Kramer came to visit you. He said you told him to kill me."

"He's lying. I never told him. I told him I was innocent."

Artemis' voice shook horribly. Her father had built a life on lies. Built a life on deceiving anyone he could get to listen to him. Over time, after enough fibs had been spewed, she simply couldn't trust a word he said. If Helen was alive...

But she didn't dare believe it.

Helen had vanished… Other girls like Helen—smart, intelligent, attractive—had slowly disappeared. Two years before he'd been arrested, her father had started his spree with his own daughter. And now here he was, lying to her again. No remorse. No apology.

Not that it would have mattered.

But she'd lost her father fifteen years ago, too. Her sister… her brother who'd run away.

And this man, behind the glass, this shapeshifting gargoyle of a man, who played with emotions like Tinker-Toys, was a constant mockery to everything she'd ever suffered.

"Maybe… maybe I can earn your trust, my dear," her father said slowly.

"Nothing you say will ever make me trust you."

"Come closer… Come on… I have something for you."

Artemis remained rooted to the spot.

He shook his head in scorn. "Fine. Fine then—if you don't want to save them. See if I care. It isn't like anyone in that damn town cares for me anyway. To hell with them. And with you." He nodded promptly, turned, and said, "Max—I think we're done here."

She stared as her father no longer looked in her direction. Refusing to make eye contact. He remained turned, waiting impatiently for the cuffs to be removed from his wrists.

The guard hesitated but then sighed, stepping forward, key in hand. "Back straight, eyes ahead," Max snapped.

Her father complied, slowly, like a man in a barber's chair.

She wanted to march away. Wanted to leave this cursed place behind. She let out a huff of air in frustration. He was playing with her. She knew that.

Save a life? Helen was dead. Helen *had* been dead for seventeen years. Her father had killed Artemis' fifteen-year-old sister.

And now he was playing games, rubbing it in her face for the fun of it.

And yet...

Standing there...

The questions whispered. *What if? What about?*

She gritted her teeth. "I'll never trust you," she blurted out.

Her father looked slowly up, his eyes locking on hers. He didn't so much smile as communicate amusement with the glint in his eyes. Like a cobra who'd finally managed to coax the mouse into its coils.

Again, all she wanted to do was turn and run.

But again...

She'd ignored her father before.

He'd told the FBI he *knew* who the killer in Pinelake was. But she hadn't believed him. In the end, it turned out he'd been telling the truth. Erik Kramer had visited the Ghostkiller in prison for tips, strategies... a sort of mentorship in murder.

So what if he wasn't lying again?

What if Helen really was alive?

"How do I save her?" Artemis said firmly. "You want to earn my trust? Tell me the truth."

He watched her for a moment, his cuffs still being unhooked from the metal bar. A tongue darted out, just barely, wetting his lips. Then, in a slow, croaking voice, he murmured, "Ten of them..."

"What?"

"Not save *her*. Save ten of them."

"Ten? Wh... where's Helen?" Artemis demanded.

"That, I don't know."

"You just said—" She began to raise her voice but then cut herself off at a sharp look from the guard by the wall.

Her father was shaking his head, though, rising to his feet. "I don't know where Helen is. You have to find who kidnapped her—then you'll find the *real* Ghostkiller. The one who killed all those poor, poor women. It... it was so horrible," he said. Tears now streamed down his cheeks. "Dear God... what a mess. What a horrible, sad, sad mess. I wish..." he swallowed. "I wish I'd raised you better, Art. I really do. I'm deeply, *deeply* sor—"

"Cut it out," she snapped. She realized in that moment, an apology would only make her hate him more. Even the tears were offensive. Pretend. Play. Had he wept as he'd strangled those teenage girls? The oldest victim had been twenty. Had he wept as he'd killed his own daughter and dumped her body in the mountains? Had he wept when he'd been taken away, led past his children?

No. None of it. He hadn't said a word at the time. His eyes cold, indifferent, calculating as ever.

But now... the tears came quickly. One of the guards was trying to push him now, guiding him back towards the door.

"One moment," Artemis said, firmly.

The guards, though, shook their heads. "Time's up," Max retorted.

"I'm with the FBI!" she snapped back. This was a bold lie. But Agent Forester *had* set this meeting up.

The guards hesitated. One of them frowned, pressing a button on a walkie-talkie.

She took the moment to step towards the glass again. The tears had evaporated on her father's cheeks once more. "Allow me to earn your trust," he whispered. "Then you'll believe me. You'll save Helen. You'll save me."

She wanted to say something scathing. To snap at him. Instead, she simply lingered. "Save ten... how?"

"Not Helen," he whispered. "I... I don't know who took her. But... but listen, Artemis, until you believe me, until you promise me you know I'm innocent, we won't talk about your sister. Understand?"

"If she really was alive," Artemis said, coldly, "A real father would want her safe. He wouldn't *use* her for leverage."

Her father snorted. "Real or *not*. I am your father. Ten victims. He's going to kill ten. Young women. Understand me?" His fingers were now tapping against the table. The guards were pulling him away once more.

The one named Max was saying something firmly, but Artemis ignored this.

"Ten... what are you talking about?"

"A killer, Artemis."

"Where? Outside?"

He grinned, nodding at her. "Yes, yes. Outside."

"How do you know? Did someone else visit you?"

He shook his head. "No... No, but... I dreamed it, Artemis. In my sleep, the third-eye whispered. Please... please believe me!"

She snorted in disgust, shaking her head. "Do you ever stop lying?"

"Do you believe I'm innocent?" he retorted.

"No."

"Same answer. Truth isn't working—I'll use what I must. And I *am* telling you the truth, my dearest baby girl. He's going to kill ten. In fact..." her father nodded, his eyes wide as he was finally pushed back towards the open, metal door. He nodded as he left, his curls swishing across his forehead. "He's already killed someone. I promise you that. Look beneath the docks. Hear me? Look beneath the docks on the lake by the red barn! I mean it, Artemis! I'm innocent. I'll prove—"

But the door shut with another loud *buzz.* The guards disappeared along with the prisoner between them.

And Artemis stood alone in the dark, dingy visitor's room, shivers trembling down her spine.

3

Rain gently pattered against the asphalt, thickening the air. Artemis shifted nervously inside her rented vehicle. She hated driving. Hated cars. And hated the insistence that something was wrong with her for wanting to avoid the highway.

She had been staying in the only hotel in Pinelake leading up to the meeting with her father. Partly, in order to hear what he had to say and partly, so that her brother, Tommy, wouldn't hate her completely. She had left Pinelake so long ago; over time, she had avoided contacting anyone back home.

Her brother, though, resented her for it. Granted, she felt it was a bit self-righteous for someone involved in the Seattle mob to accuse her of making bad choices. But when had family ever been easy?

And now, her fingers drumming against the steering wheel, she wished she hadn't stayed.

Raindrops continued to thrum, sluicing down the glass and pooling along the metal to puddle beneath the bumper. Across from her, she watched figures move in the diner, occasionally glancing out at the rain, before deciding to order an extra cup of coffee or plate of food. Rosa's diner was something of a legend in Pinelake. The pecan pie was to die for.

And according to her father, people were dying. Though not by consuming pie.

She watched as a sleek, black vehicle with tinted windows suddenly pulled off the main street, swerving into the parking lot. She felt her heart skip. This was it. Her phone buzzed. A single word from a number she had never saved but still had in her call history.

Here, the text message said.

She rolled down her window, halfway, wincing as a few droplets splashed inside the vehicle and began dripping along the plastic armrest.

The sedan moved closer, headlights flashing. A window rolled down, and a figure peered out at her.

"Miss me already?" Agent Forester said, grinning.

Another man was sitting in the passenger seat. Agent Wade. He was still wearing his sunglasses, despite the overcast skies. His suit threatened to pop a button thanks to his thick chest and broad shoulders.

Her eyes moved back to Forester. The man was somewhat hunched in the driver's seat. This, perhaps, was on account of how tall he was. At least six foot four. He also had wild, unkempt hair, which occasionally jutted straight up. The man had buttoned his suit jacket but in the wrong buttons, which she was able to tell, even sideways, thanks to the way part of the suit bulged at the collar.

She remembered when he had interrupted her finals chess match. At the time, he had been wearing mismatched socks.

"Thanks for coming," she said, her voice shaking. "I didn't know who else to call."

Wade muttered, "Police."

Artemis shook her head. "The police in this town don't like my family."

Forester emphatically and intentionally rolled his eyes. "Don't mind Wade, he's just in a bad mood. I interrupted him from a lap dance at a strip club." Forester winced and lowered his voice, "He was trying to earn a quick buck."

Wade said, "There was no stripper." He spoke with something of a resigned sigh.

Artemis knew better than to take Forester at his word. The man had something of an unusual personality. She'd witnessed the strange dynamic between the mischievous agent and his stoic partner.

According to Forester, he was ataraxic. She hadn't been able to find much on the condition. But in a few choice psychologist's journals, they suggested that people with antisocial personality disorder didn't feel social fear the same way as others.

Forester, according to his own partner, was a sociopath.

He had also saved her life.

Now, Forester was peering through the window, blinking back the occasional speckle of rainwater, and watching her. His expression morphed from mischievous to serious in an instant. Briefly, she was reminded of her father's own control of his emotions. She shivered at the recollection of the memory.

"On the call, you said you had a tip on a murder. Where?" Forester said.

Wade was still shaking his head and muttering. Artemis knew it wasn't exactly protocol to call an FBI agent on his personal number. She hadn't known they were stationed in Seattle. It had been the only choice she could think of. Sheriff Dawkins, and the rest of the police department in Pinelake, would never take a tip from Artemis seriously.

Now, though, she continued to drum her fingers against the rubber of the steering wheel. "He said beneath the dock. He mentioned a red barn. They turned it into an apple orchard. The barn is now blue, but I think I know what he meant. It's private property, though. So..." She trailed off and winced.

Another fleck of water spattered on the very edge of the half-raised window, tapping against her forearm.

Forester nodded. "All right, we'll follow you. Lead the way."

Wade said, louder, "We've only got an hour. Grant is going to notice us missing."

Artemis nodded quickly. "Thank you for coming," she said. "I owe you one."

Forester shot her a look through the open window. He winked once. "We all need friends. Lead the way, Checkers."

He was already rolling his window up, though, so he didn't hear her muttered response of, "It's chess. It's always been chess."

But then she pulled out of the parking spot, moving away from the silhouettes in the diner window, and turned onto the main road, leading the FBI agents towards the small apple orchard and the private docks for the gated community. It was the only spot she could think that fit her father's ominous description.

Ten of them. Ten victims?

Her father had been intentionally coy. But if he knew something, like last time, she couldn't avoid the clue just because the source was noxious.

On top of that, she was growing tired. Tired of the lies, of the hopes.

Her sister was dead.

If you really thought that, why are you going along with this?

She ignored the small voice in her head, scowling through the waving windshield wipers, eyes on the road. She wasn't following a lead from her father out of anything except a sense of due diligence. She had stayed a week in Pinelake to speak with the man. At least something valuable could come of it. He was silver haired, now, but the same charlatan he had always been. The same liar. She couldn't believe he'd been trying to convince her he was innocent.

She'd seen the evidence. Mountains of it. He had once literally been recorded on video sleeping next to one of the victims he had strangled. Snuggling with her corpse.

Artemis shivered in repulsion at the memory. They had matched the prints of his hands to the bruises on the victim's neck. Had shown a video of him picking the woman up outside the library. Mountains of evidence had convicted her father.

And yet it was credit to who he was that simply insisting his innocence was wearing on her mind. She knew he was lying. But her emotions wanted to think otherwise. He often played other people's emotions, pitting their intelligence against their feelings.

She hated him for it. She didn't want to follow any leads he provided. But if she didn't, and if women died, she would be responsible.

She let out a faint huff, watching the dark clouds roll over the lake. She picked up the speed, hastening towards the apple orchard. It was autumn, so the place would still be in business. Not during a rainstorm, but hopefully, she thought, it would mean there would be someone who could let them into the private estate.

Check the docks. That's what her father had wanted.

One of them was already dead. That's what he said. Ten victims, and one already dead. At the docks.

She shivered as she sped through the rain-slicked streets.

***

Agents Forester and Wade followed close behind, wincing and ducking against the downpour. Now the water came in sheets, disturbing the surface of the lake and sending the blue waters in constant vibration.

Artemis kept her black umbrella unfolded above her. Forester and Wade, though, had opted for a briefcase and a flat newspaper to protect them from the deluge.

Neither option was helping very much judging by the darkening stains on their gray suit jackets. She moved along the sodden docks, the mealy, moldered wood soft beneath her footfalls. Artemis' fingers trailed against a wooden post, and she peered along the docks where a few boats swayed with the motion of the water.

The footsteps of the agents behind her thumped against the pier. Wade had been scowling the entire trip over. But to his credit, she hadn't seen him send any text messages. As insufferable as Forester could sometimes be, Agent Wade clearly wasn't the tattling type.

Following a lead from the Ghostkiller's daughter was clearly Forester's idea.

And it was the tall, handsome agent holding a newspaper over his head who shouted, "See anything?"

Artemis shook her head, glancing into the boats. Most of them were pristine, white, with tarps unfurled to protect the interiors from the rain.

Artemis thought she spotted figures moving about inside the large barn. Likely, some of the boat owners, stopping off for a bite to eat and waiting for the storm to clear.

Forester reached the edge of the pier, glancing into the water, one hand still holding the newspaper high. This hand was calloused and displayed scars. It also had a very thick, roping scar along the palm, running up past the elbow. She knew that Agent Forester had once been a prize fighter in his youth. According to some of his younger fans, Forester was famous for having had his arm broken in a fight and then knocking his opponent out with his other arm.

He owned a gym in the city, which he ran in his spare time. She'd seen him hand out business cards before, to criminals.

He was a strange amalgam of eccentricities.

But without him, she wouldn't be alive. He had saved her from Erik Kramer the week before.

She still was having nightmares. Every night, remembering the way Kramer's face had appeared over the edge of the cliff. The knife in his hand. His unhinged voice and desperate shouting.

Forester was shaking his head and murmuring something. The sound of his words, though, was lost in the noise from the rain.

Wade had stepped onto one of the boats, peering inside but shaking his head. Artemis scanned the shoreline, feeling very silly all of a sudden. Instead of sand, black and beige seashells had been imported and scattered across the ground. The lake water lapped against the shells, swishing through and occasionally carrying some of them out into the depths.

And that's when Artemis saw it.

Coming across the water, moving slowly. A red kayak. No one paddling it. She frowned, staring.

Forester had noticed too and was scowling in the direction of the approaching vessel.

Wade, who had been busy checking another boat, pushed off, staring, his expression as grim as ever. This time, at least, his sunglasses were raised to perch on his forehead.

All three of them, trembling, shivering, and mostly soaked, stared at the approaching kayak.

Artemis didn't want to look inside. She felt a strange premonition. Her father's words came back like slick oil in her ears. She wanted to forget everything that Otto had told her. Wanted to forget his warning. His lies... the information about the murders had come in a *dream...* Yeah right. She'd have to ask Forester to check the visitor's logs.

Her father was clearly lying, but said he was trying to rebuild trust. To prove he *wasn't* a liar.

That ship had sailed, though. But while he was lying about his source of information, it didn't mean he was lying about murders in Pinelake. Seattle was considered the serial killer capital of the United States. There were more serial killers in the Pacific Northwest per capita, than almost anywhere else in the world.

It was something of a cultural fascination. A fetishization. Her father was just another in a slew of psychopaths who had exacted their hatred on society.

And so what if he was right about another one in the same town?

What if he was the one sending them here?

This thought sent another round of shivers down her back. It made sense, in a way. Erik Kramer had visited the Ghostkiller in prison and months later, went on a killing spree of his own. Otto Blythe had killed seven women nearly two decades ago. And those were just the ones that had been proven.

Her father was playing games within games. He had told Kramer to kill his daughter. She had survived, and he had denied it.

And now, as the front of the kayak slowly bumped against the wooden dock, Artemis went as still as a grave.

The two FBI agents approached slowly, hands tentatively hovering near their waists. The trees along the shore shook and swayed, shedding weaker leaves in the rain, and dropping their foliage onto the lake.

The two agents stared into the kayak, both frowning.

Summoning her courage, Artemis followed, peering into the vessel.

She frowned too.

Drenched now, water slipping past her fingertips and drip, drip, dripping to the ground, Artemis was shivering from the cold just as much as her anticipation.

But there was nothing to anticipate. The kayak was empty.

She let out a soft shivering sigh of relief. She stared into the kayak, her eyes glazing the wood, a single oar wedged against one of the seats. Nothing. Abandoned. She glanced across the lake, frowning.

Forester grunted, shaking his head in frustration, his bedraggled hair now plastered to his head. The tall, lanky FBI agent reached out with one long leg and shoved the kayak, trying to push it along the edge of the dock towards the shore now.

And suddenly, Wade snapped, "Don't!"

Artemis and Forester froze. They followed the surly agent's glare. And suddenly, the shivers from the cold turned to prickles of terror. Artemis stared into the water, her mouth open.

A young woman was in the water, staring up. Her arms were spread, her legs too, her golden hair, like a halo, swishing on the current. She wore pale, gossamer clothing, which fluttered like seaweed just beneath the surface of the water. In fact, her whole body was only a couple of inches under the liquid.

It took Artemis a second to notice the wire hooked through the woman's abdomen. Barely visible, and she wouldn't have noticed it if not for the way the wire jutted out of the liquid, broken and twisted.

She glanced sharply at the kayak and realized, in horror, the young woman had been lashed to the bottom of the vessel; when Forester had kicked it, it must've dislodged the wire.

Artemis gaped, willing the young woman to move.

Her eyes were open, her features frozen in time. Two inches below the lake surface, arms spread, hair and gossamer clothing fluttering, she looked like some ancient queen.

Very ancient, in fact. Because one thing was certain.

The girl in the water was dead.

Artemis let out a shivering breath. Her father had been right. He had even known where.

"Ten of them," she murmured beneath her breath.

Forester didn't hear. He was already barking instructions at Wade. The other agent was on his phone, calling in backup, paramedics, forensics.

Forester leaned over the water, staring at the mesmerizing way the young women floated and then began to slip, no longer attached to the kayak, and drop back below the lake.

The tall agent made a split-second decision, cursing and reaching out, lunging to snatch the descending figure. He grabbed her arm, holding her up above the water.

Artemis stared, shivering as she watched.

She wanted to hide. Wanted to cry.

Once again, she found herself smack dab in the center of a murder. Her father had been telling the truth. That didn't mean he'd been telling the truth at other times. But he'd been telling the truth now. So did that mean Helen was really alive?

Her father was the killer. He was pretending like he was innocent and trying to use Helen to do it.

But both things didn't have to be true. Maybe he was lying about the innocence. The evidence was too much. But what if he was telling the truth about Helen?

For the first time in years, despite herself, despite her best efforts, Artemis felt a small flutter of excitement. Hope.

But the hope vanished a second later, as, cursing, Forester shouted, "Give me a hand."

He had already taken one, in fact. He had grabbed the victim by the arm and was holding the corpse in place so it wouldn't dip below the water. He gestured urgently towards Artemis. Wade was still on the phone.

She wanted to refuse. But Forester was still gesturing. She let out a faint sound and then stumbled forward, dropping to a knee and reaching into the water to help pull the victim from the lake.

Her skin prickled, and her horror met a sudden surge of grief.

The woman was so young. So beautiful.

And so very, very dead.

4

"How the hell did you know she was there?"

Agent Grant's voice shook the air, and the woman with the snow-white hair stalked back and forth, her heels clicking against the straw-scattered floorboards. Grant always cut an impressive figure in Artemis' assessment, but now, she was particularly stunning.

The FBI supervising agent wore a shimmering purple dress, just shy of form-fitting. It hung past her knees but not by much. She had gorgeous, diamond earrings, which swished with her movement. The last time Artemis had seen the woman's earrings, they had been emeralds.

Grant's perfect hair didn't have a strand out of place.

She strode back and forth, shaking a finger at the roof of the barn. Artemis detected the faint scent of caramel, cider, and hay. Her nose itched thanks to this last one.

She sat miserably in a wooden chair, with Agent Forester next to her, and Wade on the other side of his partner.

Twice now, Forester had tried to get to his feet, and twice now, he had been yelled at.

So now, all three of them sat, each miserable, dripping, sodden. Water puddled beneath them. The apple orchard had been cleared nearly half an hour ago when the police had arrived.

Artemis could hear voices, shouting, rapid footsteps, as police attempted to avoid the rain while recovering the body and photographing the crime scene.

The owners of the apple orchard hadn't been happy with the developments. The boats weren't allowed to be removed either. Which had been met with much grumbling from some of the wealthier patrons.

But Grant, like a queen to her subjects, had issued commands and orders without taking feedback.

And now she had a new domain.

The effect was somewhat ruined by the caramel apples and the corn maze. But Artemis still wanted nothing more than to hide behind one of the hay bales.

"Did that sound rhetorical to you?" Grant yelled, shouting at Artemis now.

Forester said, "It did not."

Grant glared at him. "You're not funny, Cameron. Not funny at all. Why did you come here without my approval?"

Forester glanced at Grant then looked at Artemis; then shrugged. "She's hot."

Artemis held back an exasperated huff. Sometimes, the lanky agent *really* couldn't read a room.

Grant glared murderously, her eyes narrowing. "Thin ice, Cameron. You hear me? Very thin ice."

Forester shrugged. Then, seemingly realizing this wasn't the gesture she was looking for, he nodded, looking sufficiently chagrined and staring at the ground.

Grant wasn't buying it for a second, but her ire moved to Artemis now. "How?" she repeated, firmly. "I have half a mind to arrest you right now. How did you know there was a body on the lake?" Rhetorical or not, Grant didn't give Artemis a chance to reply. She was muttering now, shaking her head. "A news team is *already* here. In the rain. Don't answer any questions to the press—do you hear me?"

Through the open door, Artemis thought she spotted a pale van with the letters *IB-News,* printed in blue, on the front. A woman was standing beneath an umbrella, though, the rain was lifting. Another figure sat in the driver's seat, their breath fogging the glass as they stared in excitement towards the police. A camerman was trying to push past a police barricade but being held back.

The whole thing was turning into the exact sort of spectacle Grant didn't want.

"How did they get here so fast?" Forester muttered, staring through the door.

"Local cops," Wade replied. "They must have told them. The press arrived at about the same time." His eyes darted to Artemis, and he cleared his throat. He didn't add anything else, but Artemis could tell what he was thinking. More trouble with the local sheriff and his family because of *her*.

"Artemis?" Grant said, turning again with a frown. "I'm waiting. *How?*"

Artemis let out a shaky breath. "My father."

"Excuse me?" Those diamond earrings were mesmerizing.

"My father," Artemis said quickly. "I spoke with him. He knew she was going to be here."

Grant stiffened. She stared at Artemis. Her eyes narrowed. "I was at an event, in my honor for nearly forty years of faithful service. And now I'm dragged here, back to this horrible town, to find out that you *visited your father*? Wasn't that the one thing you refused to do last time I was in this hellhole?"

Forester nodded. "It was. You're right, boss."

"Stop agreeing with me, Cameron. You're still on thin ice."

Forester, who struggled deeply to keep his thoughts to himself, said, chipper as ever, "No more agreeing. Got it."

Wade was rubbing at the bridge of his nose, silent as ever. His sunglasses had returned to their normal spot.

Artemis was trembling, dripping, and scared. She heard more sirens behind her. The sound of tires crunching against gravel. Vehicles pulled into the parking spot outside the barn.

"I don't know how he knew," she murmured. "He told me there was going to be a body here. He said," she hesitated and glanced at Forester but continued, "said there were going to be ten more of them."

Grant stared; her pale hair almost matched the color of her face now. The blood left the woman's cheeks. She shook her head, scowling. "Ten?"

"No, sorry," Artemis said quickly. "Ten total. He seems to think there's a serial killer in Pinelake who's just getting started."

Agent Grant rubbed her face, exhaling warily. She adjusted the hem of her dress and then said, through pursed lips, "Did he say anything else?"

"Just that we would find something at the docks outside the barn. I don't know how he knew."

Grant nodded. "Wade, you're going to speak with Otto Blythe."

Wade nodded, pushing from his chair. She pointed at him. "And next time my nephew has a harebrained idea, run it by me first. Or you're fired."

Wade didn't react. He just nodded again. He then turned and moved away.

"Sorry," Forester called after his partner.

Wade remained stiff and marched back out into the rain.

Artemis was glancing at Forester now. She had wondered why Grant often used the Agent's first name. The two of them seemed very familiar. Grant had also been aware that Forester was a sociopath, but it hadn't bothered her to hire him. She had wondered at their connection, and now it made sense. Family. This was Forester's aunt.

But if she'd thought that was going to spare him a tongue lashing, Artemis was sorely mistaken.

"Cameron, please," Grant said, pleading, "I'm trying, dear. I really am trying. But you're making this so very hard. There are standards. You understand, yes?"

Forester hesitated. "No?"

"You can agree with me now."

"All right. Yes. Standards. Got it. Never break them again, swear it on my life. Swear it on my son's life."

"You don't have a son. And even if you did, I wouldn't believe you." She sighed, shaking her head. "Part of me almost wished I didn't know about all of this. But," she said, her voice trailing off, "I'm going to have to make a report. And it's going to be asked why the FBI showed up on the say-so of some civilian. If I tell them the reason was because my nephew thought she *was hot*," Grant said, her eyes like chips of ice. "I can't promise it will go over well."

Forester shifted uncomfortably, still dripping, his hair, amazingly, still unkempt despite the water. "Maybe, you can omit that part?" he said with a wince and a shrug. He didn't seem at all embarrassed that Artemis was sitting right there as he talked about her like this.

She wasn't sure if the man was joking, or if he was just being his usual self.

If anything, she owed Forester. So why did it feel so much like she wanted to strangle him?

"You were a consultant last week," Grant said, glancing at Artemis. "Which means, we just forgot to keep you on payroll. Because, as we both know, you had agreed to work with us for the month."

Artemis hesitated.

Forester turned, beaming at her.

"The month?"

Grant waved a hand, her long, perfectly manicured nails twirling. "Until the end of the month. At least that way, I can say we intended to take a case, and one of our consultants had a lead that she was following. If not ..." Grant trailed off, shaking her head in frustration and marching back and forth again across strands of scattered straw against wooden floorboards.

"I don't want to consult," Artemis said. "I'm leaving Pinelake. I was just here for the week."

"We could just arrest you, if you prefer," Grant said conversationally. She didn't even blink, beginning to nod now and murmuring, "Yes. Actually, maybe that would work. If we said we were investigating—"

"No, that's okay, I'll consult," Artemis said quickly. She had grown accustomed to Agent Grant's forms of inciting participation from others. She didn't much like it. Grant saw people as tools and decided how best to use them. She was going to bat for her nephew, but Artemis couldn't shake the thought that if Forester wasn't good at his job, Grant wouldn't have cared for him nearly so much.

"I don't know what I'm supposed to do," Artemis said, slowly.

Grant looked at her. "We'll pay you this time. It isn't like you didn't help on the last case." She sighed. "This will be the last time."

Artemis didn't reply.

"But, of course, if your father was the source of this information, you're going to have to speak with him again, but this time somewhere where I control the room."

"Wait, what? I don't want to speak with him again."

Grant said, "Too bad." She pointed a finger. "You're going to speak with him. That's the deal."

"That's what he wants," Artemis protested. "You can't move him. Leave him in that prison."

Grant hesitated. "Why shouldn't we move him?"

Artemis could feel her own anxiety rising. "It's exactly the sort of thing he would want. He's probably up to something. Maybe he has someone on the outside, ready to ambush the truck. Maybe he has someone on the local police force, who's going to slip him a key. I don't know. But he has a plan. He is playing us. He's been playing us since last week. You can't trust him."

Grant looked her directly in the eyes.

"Did he tell you where to find the body?"

Artemis hesitated but then, grudgingly said, "Yes."

"Then," she said, slowly, "I don't care what else he's up to. If he can help us find who did this to that poor girl, we'll use whatever tools we can."

Artemis pushed out of her chair, still damp, standing in a puddle of lake water. She shivered slightly but glared directly at the supervising agent. "You shouldn't move him. It's too dangerous."

Grant hesitated, bit her lip, then said, "All right. You'll interview him at that prison. But I'm going to make sure they give me a copy of all recordings and video. We won't move him. But you will speak to him again. As a consultant."

Artemis flung out her hands but shrugged. It wasn't like she had a say in the matter. Grant, at least, could be reasonable when she wanted to. She was good at taking input from all comers. Even someone she didn't trust, like Artemis. She knew, as she stood there between the two FBI agents, that she should be glad she'd won that small battle. Her father wanted to be taken out of prison. Or at least, he wanted something adjacent. She could never tell with her old man, not until it was too late.

One thing she was determined to do, though: guarantee her own father remained behind bars for the rest of his life. If that meant she had to talk to him back at that stupid prison, then so be it.

She wanted to feel defiant. Confident. But all she felt was cold and sad. And scared. She had a tournament to prepare for. She wanted to leave Washington State and never look back.

The last conversation with her father had ended up with a girl dead. She didn't want to think what a new one would entail, especially with the FBI in the room.

The feds had a way of interjecting themselves into the Blythe family affairs.

The last time they had, her brother had been led away in cuffs for a crime he hadn't committed.

She wondered if it was going to be her turn this time.

At least Grant didn't seem too serious about the threat of arresting Artemis.

Just then, Artemis heard a shout.

A sudden explosion of voices. And then a voice, louder than the others, bellowing, "Where's that evil, little bitch. Show me where she is. Now!"

Artemis whirled, staring towards the open doors to the barn.

She spotted three figures she recognized.

Her heart plummeted.

In the back, Sergeant Dawkins waddled forward. The man had an ample waistline and a long, drooping mustache, like a walrus. The mustache was white, though, she remembered when it had been closer to brown or even red.

Behind this man, came Ross Dawkins, a police officer, and an overall nuisance. He had tried to arrest Artemis last week. Now, he glared at her with mean eyes. Ross didn't have hair. He didn't have much of a neck either.

She wondered if he had traded both his neck and hair for an ample dose of stupid. Because if so, he'd gotten good bang for his buck.

The man who was yelling, though, was Sheriff Dawkins, the patriarch of the family, and the man who had provided Jamie Kramer with his alibi on the last case. Sheriff Dawkins was snarling as he marched through the doors now, his face red. He was also holding a shotgun, that he was busily raising, aiming towards where he spotted Artemis.

"Hey, hey, hey," Forester shouted, surging to his feet, and toppling the chair.

Grant yelled, reaching towards the black, sparkling purse at her hip. A weapon emerged.

Sheriff Dawkins pointed the shotgun at Artemis. "You killed my grandbaby," he screamed, tears streaming down his face. "You evil, demonic—"

Two gunshots.

Artemis nearly screamed. But she didn't feel pain. It took her a second to realize the shots had come from behind her.

The shotgun in the Sheriff's hand was still half raised, but he had tensed now, scowling.

Agent Forester was standing behind Artemis, arm raised to the ceiling, gun in his hand.

Artemis felt a faint trickle of dust slowly tumble past from where Forester had shot the rafters.

Forester was clicking his tongue and shaking his head side to side. "Sorry about that, but how about we keep this civil?"

The Dawkins family were reaching for their own weapons. Wade, however, having a sixth sense for danger, it seemed, had returned, and Artemis could see him jogging back across the asphalt, his own weapon in his hand. A few other police by the cars were moving over as well. A mixture of locals and FBI.

Artemis could feel half the eyes on her, and the other half on Forester.

She wanted to disappear. Again. But again, like every other time today, she didn't get her wish.

Forester lowered his weapon and shot Grant a look. His aunt had closed her eyes and was massaging them, muttering to herself and shaking her head side to side.

The sheriff said, "You better put that pea shooter away, boy, or I'm going to stick it someplace you don't like." The sheriff's words were replaced a second later by grumbling and cursing from Ross. The mean-eyed, thick necked police officer was gripping his own weapon.

But now, Agent Wade had emerged in the door. "Don't," Wade snapped. His hand was on his weapon now, too.

"I didn't do it," Artemis said, hoping she could help. But she should have just remained silent. Her words only seemed to provoke the Dawkins family. The Sheriff, the sergeant and the officer all began shouting at her. The hatred was palpable. Blood vessels bulged. Faces turned red. Weapons were gripped. The shotgun still faced the floor.

Artemis thought she had found herself smack dab in the middle of a national news story about to happen. She could picture the headlines now. None of them consisted of words that didn't include things like, *bloodbath, shootout, dead chess master.*

At least she had won Regionals. The national tournament, she supposed, would be harder to compete in with bullet wounds.

Finally, Grant shouted, her voice loud and commanding, "You, sir, are threatening an FBI consultant. You should be *thanking* her. She's the one who helped locate your granddaughter. I understand it's a hard time for you right now. So maybe we should keep the weapons out of it."

The woman with the white hair stalked forward and came to a stop in front of Artemis. Artemis found she could breathe a bit easier, now that Grant had positioned herself between her nephew, Artemis, and the angry police officers.

The tension was still thick. The rain continued the drum just outside the doors. Everyone was somewhat wet, tired, and angry.

"Consultant?" The sheriff snapped. "I thought you told me that was just for a couple of days."

Grant shook her head. "We extended the contract. We had reason to believe there was another killer active. And, as she has proven today, there is."

Ross Dawkins was shaking his head, scowling. "She killed my sister. *You* killed my sister!" he yelled, spittle flying as he addressed Artemis.

Forester muttered, "Why do these guys think you killed her?"

Artemis tried not to move her lips as she whispered back, "Sheriff Dawkins lost his first wife to my dad."

Forester winced, nodding. He slowly lowered his gun, slipping it into his holster. "See," he called, louder, "we can all just get along."

Artemis didn't feel particularly noble, cowering behind the two feds, but she also had no interest in emerging to face their accusations. She lingered in the back, in the shadows, her heart in her throat, and her hands twisting nervously.

The tension lingered, dark looks cast about. The officers all glared at her, clearly imagining what her body might look like with ventilation. But now, with an audience, with the FBI lingering, Sheriff Dawkins snorted once. He jammed a finger towards her and said, scowling, "If I see you around town..."

"You'll do nothing," Grant insisted.

Dawkins just muttered, shaking his head. His son, the sergeant, had tears of rage in his eyes, his hands bunched. He turned, following after his father as the two of them moved back in the direction of the coroner's van.

Artemis watched them leave, still shivering, but this time not due to the cold.

"Let's get going," Forester murmured at her side. "Probably best we don't linger." He tugged at her arm insistently, leading her quickly towards a side exit door marked by a bright, red sign.

Grant didn't protest, still massaging her temples. Agent Wade stood in the door, watching Forester's back and waiting until the two of them exited out the side before setting off once again.

Another murder. Another case.

She'd returned to Pinelake, and now it had its hooks in her.

She shivered, trembling in frustration as Forester pulled her quickly along. "Gonna speak with the coroner while he works on the body," Forester muttered. "Wade will set up the new interview with your old man. Just... just try not to get shot, okay?"

"No promises," Artemis muttered, wondering if perhaps she should call Tommy. Maybe... Jamie? The last time she'd spoken with Jamie, though, she'd accused him of murdering his own mother.

And then, it had turned out, Jamie's *father* was a serial killer.

Artemis' stomach twisted at the thought.

Jamie had been the only warmth in a cold town. And she'd ruined that too. Her brother... Tommy was a criminal. He hated Pinelake.

No... no, she couldn't go running to someone else to solve her problems.

She'd been the one to decide to visit her father in prison. And now she was reaping the reward.

"D-do you know where the coroner's is?" Artemis asked.

"Yeah — got it on GPS. Here, my car's the black one. I'll drive. Try... try not to soak the seats *too* badly. Just got them cleaned."

This request, like everything else today, felt as if it were very much beyond Artemis' control.

Wet seats, dead girls, mentalists behind bars...

She was being tossed by choppy waves, manipulated.

But she couldn't say exactly *why.*

What did her father want?

The coroner wouldn't have these answers... At least, she didn't think so. But it was as good a place as any to start the hunt.

5

The coroner's office wasn't nearly as dingy or cold as Artemis had expected. She certainly hadn't been anticipating the colorful paintings and brightly-hued motivational posters lining the hallway leading to the coroner's office.

One poster read:

Some heroes make it up the mountain. Some out of the chasm.

Another one, with a brightly colored rainbow fluttering over a castle, read: *Some say don't get your hopes up. I say don't let your despairs get you down.*

Artemis moved past a large painting displaying a beautiful vista of some sunny beach overlooking crashing waves. She smiled, thinking of California, where she'd lived for the last ten years. Salinas, a small town not much different than Pinelake in some ways.

But polar opposites in others.

As Artemis followed Forester towards the opaque door at the end of the hall, the tall agent paused to read another poster, which read, *The world is full of kindness. If you don't see it, be it.*

Forester scratched at his chin. He glanced down the hall, confused, then back at the door, double-checking the name on the glass.

It read *Dr. Miracle Bryant, Coroner.* Someone had added glitter to the sign.

"Umm... this is the right place?" Artemis murmured.

Forester scratched at one of his lumpy ears. "I... I expected less... sparkle."

"Yeah..."

Forester sighed, shook his head but then knocked on the door, his knuckles rattling the glass. No response. So he tried the door handle, turning it slowly and pushing the door open.

Forester and Artemis both stared into the coroner's office. Music was playing from the center of the room. An up-beat, playful tone with no lyrics. And there, a round, middle-aged woman with bright, pink hair like candy floss was dancing as if her life depended on it.

Hip thrusts, sashays, swaying, disco moves and more than one twirl as she spun around and around the coroner's office.

The walls inside the office were similarly adorned to the hall, with bright colors, encouraging posters and vibrant art. Artemis watched as the round woman shook her hips side to side, paused to check something on a clipboard, then continued dancing in the other direction. She paused to pick up something metal from a tray as the music swelled. She hesitated dramatically, scowling from behind large, sparkly-framed glasses, and then when the music continued, she bent over, poking and prodding at the body on the table.

The air of excitement and energy was somewhat ruined by the corpse in the middle of the room.

Artemis' eyebrows hadn't quite reached their peak yet, and Forester was busily trying to step back, as if attempting to escape into the hall.

Artemis didn't let him, though, and instead pushed him, hands in the small of his back, shoving him into the room.

The strange contrast of the bright colors and the grim scene on that gurney was making Artemis' head spin.

Suddenly, as Dr. Miracle Bryant spun around a second time, she spotted them.

She let out a loud squeak. Dropped her clipboard. Tried to shut off the music and in doing so knocked a metal tray full of tools off the table, sending them scattering across the floor. Finally, her finger found the button on a small Mp3 player, and she clicked it off, mouth open, gaping at the two of them.

"Dear God," she said. "Oh, Jesus. Lord, help me. Did... I—hello! So sorry. So very, very sorry!" The woman was wincing and smiling and wincing and grimacing and oscillating between multiple emotions.

Her eyes permanently sparkled, and her cheeks dimpled every time she smiled and then flinched.

Forester watched her with amusement, like a customer at a movie theater. Artemis, suffering from a case of secondhand embarrassment, had already hurried forward, hitting her knees against the cold ground as she helped to pick up some of the tools.

A few of them were slick with blood. She shivered, avoiding these as best she could.

Artemis had to hand it to Dr. Bryant. Of all the things she'd been expecting to confront her at the coroner's office, this scene had not been high on the list.

Now, Dr. Bryant was hurriedly picking up some of the recovered tools, saying, "Thank you, dear. So nice. So sorry. I just — trying to get my steps in for the day. You know," she said, prattling and shaking her head to punctuate each short sentence. "New Fitbit. It does fireworks and everything when you hit your goal."

Forester was leaning back now against the doorframe, arms crossed, one eyebrow raised.

Artemis shot him a glare.

She still hadn't confronted him about his comments back in the barn. He had decided to help her because he thought she was hot? He was joking. She knew that much. But it was disrespectful. Rude. Bordering on harassment.

She was determined to give him a piece of her mind. Not yet, though.

As Artemis put the last of the metal implements back on the tray and Dr. Bryant deposited these in a sink, quickly washing her hands and using a strong-smelling disinfectant, Artemis returned to her feet, straightening.

"I didn't see you!" Dr. Bryant said, waving a hand towards the body on the gurney. "I only just got started. So sorry."

Forester called from the doorway, "No need to apologize. You have some pretty good moves."

The dark-haired woman grinned but shifted uncomfortably. Her eyes had wrinkles in the corners, and she couldn't have been much younger than fifty, but she carried herself with a vibrancy and an energy as she hurried around the table and began fidgeting with the MP3 player Artemis had spotted earlier.

"That was the song playing when... when poor Robin—oh dear. Not that it matters. Just," she winced, shaking her head. She forced a quick smile and a nod.

"Dr. Bryant," Forester cut-in, "we don't mean to rush you, but we were hoping for some preliminary help. We have an interview in an hour and wanted to go with some information."

"Perfect. Yes." Dr. Bryant hesitated, then nodded to herself. Her dark, smooth chin jutted forward, as she tilted her head back, her pink hair cascading, her eyes on the ceiling for a moment. She hesitated, wrinkling her nose, and then said, "This morning. About seven AM."

"Excuse me?" Forester said.

"Poor little Robin," said the coroner quickly. She pointed at the young woman beneath the sheet on the table. "That's when she died. Or… well when she *last* died."

"I thought you said you just started. You can already tell time of death?"

"I won't bore you with the details. But it's a combination of body temperature, how many songs were playing on the MP3 player, and Robin's usual routine, which her father was very kind to email me."

The woman spoke quickly, and every sentence was occasionally interjected with a smile, dimples flashing, eyes twinkling. But then, as if embarrassed by her smile, she would wince and look away.

Artemis was beginning to like the woman.

Not just because of the pink hair and positive attitude but also because Artemis respected competence, and this woman had managed to piece together three chains of information to find something useful.

Perhaps it was this sudden sense of camaraderie that prompted Artemis to ask, "What do you mean, when she *last* died?"

Here, Dr. Bryan's voice went cold. She looked down at the ground, frowning. "There are bruises on her chest. He administered CPR…"

"What? Who did?"

Bryant looked up.

"The killer?" Forester asked. "Why?"

Bryant sighed, shaking her head. "I'm only just getting to the lungs... but..." She gave a sad shake. "I think he drowned her, then resuscitated her, then drowned her again."

Artemis felt a sudden tremor up her spine. She stared in horror at Bryant.

"You're joking," she murmured.

"I'm afraid not in the least. Not at all."

A faint moment of horror lingered. Artemis cleared her throat, though, and pressed on. She pointed. "That's not Robin's own gown, is it?"

Dr. Bryant looked over. "I couldn't say. Why do you think that?"

Artemis indicated the MP3 player. "She was on a morning run, right?"

"Did Mr. Dawkins send you his daughter's schedule as well?"

Artemis shifted uncomfortably at the mention of the police sergeant; instead of answering, she simply said, "Which means the killer must've dressed her in that."

Forester grimaced. "Creepy," he muttered beneath his breath. He pushed off the door, looking far less amused now. He approached the gurney, frowning at the form beneath the thin sheet. "We have a cause of death?"

"Yes, I'm afraid. There's water in the lungs. But bloating. She drowned," said Dr. Bryant quickly. The twinkle had vanished from her eyes for a moment. She murmured a faint prayer, looking in the direction of the young girl.

Artemis shifted uncomfortably. Forester didn't pay attention. The woman with the bright pink hair looked up. "I'm not sure what else I can tell you. She went for a run according to her father at five AM. She was taken not long after, since the song stopped. But *killed* at seven. Which means there was a two-hour window where the killer might have gotten his hands on her."

"You think the killer took her somewhere first?" Forester said.

"It's possible. That's forensic's area of expertise. But I did find, on her bare feet, signs of red clay. That's not normally on the bike path around the lake."

Forester nodded. "You're local?"

"Only in the last few years. My husband and I moved to a smaller town for the kids." She flashed a quick smile and a nod.

Artemis suppressed a faint sigh of relief. Part of her had been concerned the coroner, like so many in Pinelake, would recognize her... and loathe her on sight. But the friendly glances and faint smiles from the pleasant, round-faced woman were a nice respite.

"Dr. Bryant," Artemis said, slowly. "Did you find any sign of sexual assault?" As she said it, she winced. Not just because of the nature of the question, but because she felt out of her depth. She was not an FBI agent. She had never wanted to be an FBI agent. And once again, she found herself as a press-ganged Fed.

Dr. Bryant said, "Call me Miracle." She gave a quick nod. Another predictable smile. Then she said, "No sign of sexual assault. I can't confirm that just yet, but preliminary indicators suggest no."

"So someone attacked her, took her somewhere, dressed her, then drowned her?" Forester asked.

The coroner nodded. "There was a piercing mark in her abdomen. It looks like a wire was pushed through her skin."

Artemis and Forester winced. Miracle said quickly, "It was post-mortem. Which just means after death—though... You two look very smart. I'm sure you knew that."

Forester nodded as if agreeing with this assessment. He said, "He used that wire to attach her to the bottom of the kayak."

The coroner wrinkled her nose. "Really? How strange. Why?"

"Hell if I know. It was raining, we saw the kayak coming towards us. As if propelled by a motor."

"But it didn't have a motor?"

"Nope."

Artemis frowned. "He must've seen us and launched it towards us from across the shore."

Forester huffed. "Which means he was close enough to catch if I had thought to do something. Dammit."

Miracle looked uncomfortable at the curse word. She was now humming something beneath her breath.

Then, quickly, the middle-aged woman's eyebrows shot up. These were also tinged pink. She said, "I don't know if it's relevant, but one of Robin's ankles is sprained."

Forester paused. "You think the killer did that?"

Artemis shook her head. In a murmur, she said something. The other two glanced at her. Artemis hesitated, cleared her throat, and, trying not to blush, said louder, "She was running from him."

These grim words seemed to sap some of the color out of the strange office space.

Artemis simply couldn't bring herself to look too closely at the body beneath the sheet. Robin would have only been eighteen. She had only been a toddler when Artemis had last been in Pinelake. And now, there she was, cold, dead.

"What about the strange outfit?" Forester said slowly. "It looked like some sort of nightgown. Maybe a wedding dress?"

Artemis shook her head. She had never seen a flowing, white outfit quite like it. Granted, Artemis bought most of her clothes online.

But the gregarious coroner shook her head. "It's homemade," she said softly. "I can spot the difference between manufactured stitch work and amateur stitch work. This gown, for whatever reason, was made by an amateur."

Forester hesitated. He shifted uncomfortably where he stood at the edge of the gurney. "The killer?"

Miracle shook her head. "I couldn't say. I might be able to get more back to you. I'll be running a toxicology report as well. Do I have your number?"

"Here, I have a business card."

But Artemis felt a slow shiver as the conversation wound to a halt.

Now, it was unavoidable. Grant wanted her back at that prison. In order to prevent them from moving her father, which she knew was a huge mistake, Artemis would have to go see him in person.

And this time, she would be accompanied by two federal agents. She could already feel a slow sense of embarrassment. Her own father... What would Forester, Grant or Wade think of her after they met Otto Blythe?

She shivered at the thought of them reading through her father's arrest reports.

As Forester traded information with the coroner, Artemis glanced along the wall, arms wrapped tight. She shivered faintly in the chilly room. On one side of the room, covered with more hotel art, there were rows of wall-to-wall, floor-to-ceiling cooling compartments.

There were only eight doors.

Not enough space, it seemed, if her father's premonition proved true.

Ten victims. Eventually, ten women would be killed. Artemis had to find who was doing this before that happened.

She frowned to herself, shifting uncomfortably. As Forester turned and began approaching her, Artemis noticed Dr. Bryant was tapping her foot and beginning to sway again with some unheard music.

Artemis admired the woman's ability to smile while working on corpses.

She could only hope that by the end of the week, Miracle would still have that twinkle in her eye.

Because if the Ghostkiller was right, then there would be little cause for joy in the coming days.

Pinelake had a strange way of attracting death.

6

Artemis found herself in the visitor's room back at the prison once more. This time, her father was sitting at one of the round, plastic tables, his hands cuffed to the surface through a steel loop coated in protective rubber. She shifted uncomfortably as her father's eyes darted between the three figures across from him.

Agent Wade had a notepad out and was scribbling on it while Agent Forester leaned back, his long legs extending casually beneath the table, his arms crossed.

Artemis bit her lower lip and tried not to let her mind dart around *too* much. Her father had recently had a meal. He had been given rec time earlier in the day. But even as she uncatalogued this information, she hesitated. The stain of gravy on his lapel didn't match with his usual care at mealtime. The air-ruffled nature of his hair looked a bit... *intentional.*

She frowned now at her father, wondering if he had the gall to intentionally mislead even these *small* observations. Had he stained his collar on purpose with a speck of food just to misdirect her? Had he tousled his hair, normally so neat, just so she would reach the wrong conclusion?

She had to remember that everything was a game with this man. And now, sitting at the plastic table in a dark, dingy visiting room in a maximum-security prison, he was playing his little heart out.

But she knew games. She shifted, her legs crossed beneath the table. She sat upright, frowning towards her father now. She refused to give him the satisfaction of even the smallest victory.

Two guards stood behind her father—different from the ones before. A third guard—the one with an upcoming wedding—stood by the door that led into the visiting room.

Her father was smiling gregariously at the two FBI agents across the table, his gaze skipping past Artemis as if she wasn't even there.

"I don't know *what* my daughter has been telling you," he said, adding a little laugh. "She has a very *wonderful* imagination, though." He leaned back slightly, his handcuffs rattling. A snake oil salesman's grin creased his lips.

Forester was smiling back, but it was more like the lupine leer of a wolf with its eyes on a mountain lion. Wade didn't find anything amusing. The man had removed his sunglasses but glared with stoic features at Artemis' father.

Wade had a sharp jaw, sharp cheekbones, and even a brow line that looked as if it had been carved from granite. He wasn't quite handsome, but he certainly wasn't ugly. He looked more like an action hero than anything.

Forester on the other hand, looked like a delinquent jammed against his will into a suit. He never could seem to figure out how to button the thing. And now, the collar was fixed, but two of the buttons at the bottom had been left un-clasped.

"Sir," Wade said, monotone as ever, "I'm not sure what you think to gain by gas-lighting your daughter. We have the security footage of your last conversation."

Seamlessly, her father moved from coy and condescending to playful and mischievous. His eyes even seemed to twinkle beneath the dull light above the table. "Just a little joke. Some prison humor for you. Of course, I'm happy to help. But I don't know what more I can tell you. The spirits visit when they like."

Artemis rolled her eyes.

Forester perked up, though. "You're a psychic?"

The eager nature of the question was like a piece of flank steak dangled before a grizzly bear. Artemis' father zeroed in on Agent Forester. It was as if no one else was in the room, save the ex-fighter with the lumpy ear and the untamed hair.

"I am," Otto said.

"He's not," Artemis interjected.

"In fact," said her father, slowly, "I think I see you, yes. I'm getting, one moment, yes, the letter C. No, wait, D. Yes, letter C or D, is that important to you?"

Artemis just watched. She had seen the show enough times that she found it all quite pedestrian.

Forester, though, was leaning forward, excited. "Yes. My name. It's Cameron. It starts with a C."

Her father nodded quickly. "I knew it. Yes, Cameron. There's a strong aura about you."

Otto nodded solemnly. Artemis snorted. Wade was still taking notes. Forester, though, looked as if he had made a new friend.

"Wait," said the agent, "can you see anything else?"

"Did you happen to," Otto said, slowly, "participate in–"

"Combat sports, yes," Artemis snapped. "It's the ear, Forester. Also, you look like a neanderthal."

"What's a nean-neand—neander—" Forester said, frowning in mock concentration.

Artemis just muttered to herself, shaking her head.

Forester gave her a glance; he kept his smile somewhat fixed but said, slowly, "We're here to solve a case. There is one woman dead; if the *spirits*," he said, gritting his teeth and emphasizing the word, "have insight, I'd like to hear it. Wouldn't you?"

She hesitated. Then shrugged sheepishly, realizing perhaps Forester wasn't quite the fool he played. Of course, he was right. The best way to get her father to talk was to play his games. But she refused to pay the price. There was always something with Otto.

"Yes, a fighter," her father said quietly. "In fact," he said, "a champion. Isn't that right? But that scar on your hand," her father continued in a slow, droning voice, intended to lull his audience, "you didn't get that in a fight. At least, not a fight in the cage."

Artemis hesitated. She glanced at Forester, who was no longer watching her but had returned his attention to her father. He said, "Wow, you have a strong gift."

Artemis glanced at the tall agent's scarred hand. She hadn't picked up on this last part. Then again, her father had years of practice more than her. Still, it was unsettling to realize he still could notice things she couldn't.

"About the girl," Wade insisted, trying to redirect.

But now Otto Blythe leaned forward, almost imperceptibly, his cuffed hands resting on the plastic table so lightly his fingers almost hovered. "Do you regret it, Agent Forester?"

"Regret what?" Cameron asked.

"Forester, let it go." Artemis shook her head. She waved towards Wade as if to give him permission to continue questioning.

But it was as if a spell were cast between the two men. Forester stared into the Ghostkiller's eyes. He shifted uncomfortably.

"I think I see it," her father whispered. "Seven years ago, wasn't it? You haven't told anyone. Not a single soul."

Artemis went rigid. Forester had gone as still as stone. His eyes fixated on her father, but his feet shuffled back, no longer crossed in an easy-going posture. He leaned forward, tense.

She knew the physical markers. Her father knew something.

Shit. Her father knew something he shouldn't. How? How could he possibly know something about an FBI agent he had never met?

"What was her name, Cameron?" The Ghostkiller whispered. He smiled now, his hazel eyes flashing. "You still miss her, don't you? You think you don't have regrets. You think because of your condition," her father said slowly, pointing both fingers towards his own head, "that you're not allowed to regret, don't you? It's important you know this, Cameron. You're human. Just like all of us. It's why you joined the FBI, isn't it? Yes, yes, I can see it now. And when you found him... because we both know you found him, didn't you, about three years ago."

"Enough," Cameron said. There was no joviality to his voice. His fists were bunched on the table.

But, of course, her father kept going. "I know what you did," he said in a singsong voice. "I know what you did. Naughty, naughty." Those two fingers which had still been pointing towards his face began to wag back and forth like a disapproving mother.

Forester's face was now blank.

Artemis snapped. "He's lying. Cameron, don't believe a word he says."

"Should I tell them?" Otto whispered. "Should I mention what happened? I've been in here. This stuff isn't on the Internet. Not even your partner, Agent Wade, knows. Do you, Wade?"

Artemis noticed how the other agent had almost imperceptibly shifted so he was poised, leaning forward, both his hands removed from the notepad now, as if ready to snatch at Forester.

Forester nodded, tight-lipped. "Well, holy shit. Call me a believer. I did tell you to stop, though." Artemis noticed his hand now bunching into a fist. She reached out, catching his elbow. "Don't," she whispered sharply.

Her father glanced at where her hand touched Forester's elbow. And then his eyes shifted to hers, holding her gaze for a second. No warmth, no mirth. The eyes of a dead man. Of a ghost.

"I told my daughter," her father said, slowly, "everything that I know. If I had anything to add, I would. But I don't."

"How did you know about the murder?" Wade said, still glancing at his partner. But Forester's hand uncurled now that the conversation had shifted. But he was still breathing heavily, his chest trembling as he tried to compose himself. Artemis had seen Forester single-handedly beat up a room of mobsters. She knew he could handle himself in a fight.

But in a place like this, with a man like that, there were certain weapons that a boxing gym didn't train.

What had her father found out? Something seven years ago? Three years ago?

Artemis could already piece together some of what he had said, given Forester's reaction.

She didn't like that she was even thinking along these lines. Anything her father said was best ignored.

She let out a faint exhale and leaned back again, closing her eyes briefly and blocking out the image of her father. The image of the guards and the prison walls.

All she could see, briefly, was the young woman, dead, floating in the lake, a wire through her stomach and gossamer strands of white lace fluttering around her.

Her father said, slowly, "I told you everything I know. You don't have to believe me, but the information came from a dream. That's it."

Wade said, "Sir, I'm going to need more than a dream."

"You checked my visitor logs, didn't you? I haven't had any in months. None, except for her," he said, nodding to Artemis.

"So how did you know about the plan to kill the police sergeant's daughter?" said Wade, still speaking monotone but beginning to show some signs of irritation.

Her father clasped his hands, shrugging a single time. His prison jumpsuit still looked as neat and clean as she noticed the first time she'd come—save a faint mark near the collar. Now, though, he said, "He's going to do it nine more times. That's all I can tell you. So if you want to stop him, you had better do something about it, instead of wasting your time here."

"What do you want?" Agent Forester said suddenly.

Her father turned again. "Excuse me?"

"In exchange for information, we can offer you better accommodations. Maybe a job in the library. What's something you want? You help us, and we help you." Artemis noticed that Forester's tone wasn't nearly so cavalier as it usually was. He was still eyeing her father with something between anger and guilt.

Otto said, "I can't think of anything I need. Well… now that you mention it. There is *one* thing."

"And what's that?" Wade replied.

He pointed a finger at his daughter. "She has to believe me. That I did not kill her sister. That I'm innocent. That I did not strangle those seven, poor, delicate, lovely, beautiful, smart young women."

Artemis could feel the blood rushing to her cheeks. Of course, he would bring it up. She couldn't quite meet Forester or Wade's gaze. The embarrassment was second only to her revulsion at the comment. Slowly, so she was certain he could hear her, she enunciated clearly. "You're a murderer," she said simply. "And you're going to spend the rest of your life in prison. Hopefully that's clear enough for you, *dad*."

And then she pushed to her feet and turned on her heel, walking away. She had heard enough. If he was going to provide something useful, he already would have. The fact that the FBI was offering the man favors in return for information boggled the mind. They clearly didn't know who they were dealing with. A master manipulator. The best place for him was smack dab in the middle of a rigid routine. No changes, no rewards. Routine.

Her father couldn't manipulate stone walls or iron bars. People, on the other hand, were his playthings. The less time she spent in a room with him, the better.

She paused by the door, waiting for the guard on the other side to notice her.

Wade was asking another question. "Is there anything else you can tell us about the murder?"

Her father said slowly, "The killer, though I can't be sure, but I think I saw it in a dream, he's..." Her father trailed off, wrinkling his nose as if in thought. "A survivor. And he is going to give his prey a fair chance. He always does. It's quite noble of him, if you think about it." Her father nodded earnestly, his eyes widening.

"Do you have a name?" Forester insisted.

"I'm sorry, now, honestly, I'm growing tired. I'll think about that trade you offered. There might be something you could do for me."

Artemis felt her skin crawl. She didn't like hearing this type of talk. It was for this very reason she had agreed to return to this prison. So they wouldn't transfer him elsewhere. She glanced up at one of the security cameras in the room, which Agent Grant had mentioned she would be watching.

The door buzzed in front of her. A *click*. The metal frame swung slowly open, and she shifted sideways, refusing to step back even an inch, to allow the door to open.

Once a small enough gap had appeared, she shoved towards it and stepped out of the visitor's room, a horrible taste in her mouth.

Her father was playing games.

But she could think of at least one way he might have contact with a serial killer.

He had mentioned that Wade probably checked the visitor's log. And if it was true that no one had recently visited, and barring any red flags from previous visitors, like Mr. Kramer, then there was only one other pool to look at.

Prisoners.

Friends, cellmates, and the like. Especially any that had recently been released.

She nodded to herself. Her father had gone to great lengths to try and convince them that the source of his information wasn't proximate. Which meant, the exact opposite was likely true.

Maybe it was a prisoner who he had shared a room with. Maybe it was someone he had overheard in the library or in the showers. Maybe, she considered as she waited for the guard to lock the door again and escort her away, her father had put things in motion. Just like he had with Kramer.

Pinelake was the target. Her father an avenging monster.

Even behind bars, he was sending death towards her hometown. Even in prison, he was finding ways to continue his murder spree.

It was as this settled and the guard gestured at one of his colleagues to lead Artemis away, that she reached some type of certainty.

Her father would have to be stopped, if the murders in Pinelake were to be stopped. She didn't know how, yet. She didn't know what sort of levers were available to the FBI, but she was determined. He would have no more visitors. No mail. Nothing. No time with the other prisoners. At least, not until she was certain that Pinelake was safe.

The Blythe name had caused enough damage already.

And now, she was determined to rectify some of it.

7

"You're sure he had no visitors?" said Agent Grant, frowning at them.

They were once again back in the large, apple orchard barn. It wasn't quite a police precinct, but given the last interaction with local law enforcement, Agent Grant had decided the best place to set up a base of operations was a neutral location.

Every time Artemis glanced out the open wood-beam doors at the lake, she shivered. Even the beauty of the water seemed strange now.

Artemis sat on a bale of hay, watching as Forester taste-tested a caramel apple; he had also downed two cups of cider. He had been quieter than she was accustomed to ever since they had returned from the prison.

He was frowning more than she was used to as well. Wade, taking the role of spokesperson for a change, was answering Grant's questions. "I checked with both the warden and the guards. The only visitor Mr. Blythe had in the last five years was Kramer. And he's dead."

Forester held up a hand. "*Mea culpa*," he said sarcastically.

Artemis winced.

Grant glanced at her nephew. "I saw your exchange with Mr. Blythe," she said, firmly. "I'm going to ask you this once. Cameron, is there anything I should be worried about?"

Forester flashed a grin, but it didn't quite reach his eyes. "Absolutely not."

Grant sighed, shaking her head. She was still wearing that fancy purple dress. But the earrings had been removed. Now, she looked at Artemis. "You left the interrogation early."

"He was lying," Artemis said. "Like I said, he's not worth talking to."

"And yet," said Grant, "he's the best source of information we currently have. And given that, I was hoping we might have something more than hurt feelings and excuses." She frowned at each of them in turn.

Wade said, monotone, "Actually, Artemis had an idea."

Artemis looked over. She was pretty sure this was the first time Wade had used her name. The stony-faced FBI agent continued, "I looked through records of any cellmates, acquaintances, accomplices or otherwise that Mr. Blythe had in prison."

Grant nodded. "Good play. And?"

"One of them has a record," Forester said.

Grant frowned. "They're prisoners, Forester. They all have records."

"No, literally," Forester said. "He's a musician. He was released about two years ago. Large man. Big belly. He looks kind of like Santa Claus actually, from the pictures."

Grant glanced at Wade who nodded once and shrugged.

Grant tilted her head, a white curl swishing past her cheek. "And so why is this musician of interest to us?"

"He kept in touch," Artemis called out. She had also seen the information Wade had managed to finagle from the prison. "He's been sending letters to my father, right?" she added, glancing at Wade.

The agent nodded. "Letters, postcards. They don't make sense. It's a bunch of gobbledygook. We think he's writing in code."

"Well, is he?" Grant asked. This time, all three of the agents looked directly at Artemis.

She slouched on her hay bale, trying to make herself as small as possible. "I don't know yet. I haven't had time to look through. Maybe. Probably."

Grant pursed her lips and nodded a single time. "All right, well, in that case, I want to make sure that Ms. Blythe has access to those letters and notes in order to find out what he's been communicating to her father. As for this musician, what's his name?"

"Joseph Baker," said Forester. "And get this, he has a lake house."

Grant looked at least a little less disappointed now. "Do we have any other potential inmates on the outside connected with Mr. Blythe?"

Wade shook his head, rattling off as if reading lines in a play, "Baker was the only one released. The others are lifers. They don't usually mix lifers with short-term guys, but Baker was exonerated because one of the arresting officers had a record of tampering with evidence and the judge overseeing the case was feeling generous."

Grant shook her head in frustration. "And this Baker, this musician, what was he guilty of when he went away?"

"Rape, murder," said Forester. "He killed his pregnant wife and threw her in a river."

"Charming. Nice to see the justice system working." Grant let out a frustrated breath, her eyes flashing. "You two go speak to Mr. Baker. And you, Artemis, I want to know what he's been saying to your father."

Artemis held up a hand as if she were in school.

"Yes?"

"I think we should pay more attention to what my father was saying to *him*."

Wade shook his head once. "No outgoing mail. He's not allowed. I checked."

Artemis frowned. "He has to be communicating somehow."

"No mail according to the warden. Prison policy for the supermax guys."

Artemis huffed in frustration. "Do you happen to know if his cell has a window?"

Forester tapped his nose and pointed.

She continued "A window might give him an opportunity to communicate with the outside world. Maybe with lights, something one of the prisoners can see."

Agent Grant nodded. "Wade, check into that on your way to Mr. Baker's home."

Artemis stood to her feet. "I'd like to go with them."

Again, all three feds glanced in her direction. Artemis felt a couple of strands of straw flutter from the fabric of her trousers. She brushed sheepishly at her legs and straightened. She swallowed but said, "If my father is involved, then this is only his first move. He has something planned, and I want to be there to make sure he doesn't win."

"Win?" Grant said slowly.

"*Succeed*, hurt anyone," Artemis corrected quickly.

"This isn't a game, Ms. Blythe. You're aware of this?"

Grant fixed her with a very severe look. But this time Artemis didn't balk. She looked right back at the older woman and said, quietly, "Agent Grant, with all due respect, you're wrong. That's exactly what this is. To my father, this is a game. You and I, and even these women, are pieces. For us to stop him and whatever is happening outside the prison walls, I have to beat him at his own game."

Grant frowned back at Artemis. She didn't reply right away.

Forester was pushing to his feet now, having abandoned the caramel apple, and was now strolling through the open barn doors towards the waiting vehicle.

Grant shot Wade a look. "She stays in the car," she said.

Wade flashed a thumbs up.

"I mean it."

Wade nodded once. And he also pushed to his feet and turned, moving back towards the opening in the barn door. Sunlight streamed through the gap, illuminating the floorboards and catching the strands of straw with a golden glint.

Artemis' nose itched, and she wanted nothing more than to escape the barn, to breathe some fresh air.

But as she turned away from Grant as well, taking the woman's silence not so much as affirmation as permission, she couldn't shake the slow feeling of dread.

Her father, whatever he was up to, had been planning it for a while.

He was involved. She knew he was involved. She just had to find out how.

Beating him at his own game would take more than desire.

It would take everything she had learned over the last thirty years about human nature, the way people thought, and what lurked in the mind of a serial killer.

Her work was clear. And if she didn't succeed, more women would die.

8

ARTEMIS SAT IN THE backseat as they drove around the lake. She frowned at her phone, studying pictures from the prison of the strange notes that Joseph Baker had sent her father. They all started the same.

Dear GK.

Ghostkiller? She shook her head, wrinkling her nose. They all signed off the same.

Yours, JB.

Joseph Baker. That seemed simple enough.

It was the parts in between that made absolutely no sense. She frowned, reading and re-reading again. *In March. No June. Love dwindles, but how does a grocer know or grow? Seems unlikely. How I try my very best, though. Truly yours... If not, otherwise. Sunday may fail.*

And it went on like that, for paragraphs. Each postcard, nearly eighty of them. They were all more of the same. Incoherent, jumbled messes. Always addressed to *Dear GK*. And always signed, *Yours, JB.*

The postcard pictures held few clues as well. One was from Pinelake, showing the trees and the mountains. Another was from Seattle, depicting the Space Needle. Still another postcard was blank, no picture whatsoever.

Artemis shook her head, scowling as she scanned the information.

"What are you up to?" she murmured.

Her father was likely communicating in some way.

Wade and Forester were both watching the GPS in the front seat, moving slowly around the large lake. Over ten thousand acres... one of the largest lakes in the Pacific Northwest. It had many smaller tributaries and rivers.

Small clusters of homes took up portions of the shore. Many of them large, triangular, with broad windows, adorning their walls with the scenery itself.

Artemis swiped on her phone, scanning other notes but finding it difficult to make sense of any of the cards. One stood out to her, though, and she paused.

"Huh," she murmured.

Forester glanced in the mirror. "What is it, Checkers?"

"This one," she said. "It's addressed to GK, but it's signed off with JD instead of JB."

"A typo?"

"Maybe… They're handwritten." Artemis frowned, reading some of the message.

Crocodile Un. Number Uno. How? We fall. Summer. Twice Summer. Follow pencils along the orange line to the tip of the icebrg. Hahahaha. I think you know.

She wrinkled her nose. The word iceberg was misspelled. So clearly, JB wasn't *too* cautious with the phrasing of his notes. Which meant what? The sentences themselves? Something in the *type* of words used.

She skimmed further.

"Coming up ahead," Forester called.

Wade grunted. He glanced in the mirror. "Stay here," he said.

"Do I get a treat?" she muttered.

Wade ignored the jab. The GPS announced their arrival to a home on their left. Joseph Baker's house was a quaint, two-story lakeside beauty. The tranquil waters stretched before his front yard. Artemis glanced through the windshield now, peering between the trees. The rainclouds had lifted, sunlight replacing the dark, burdened skyline.

But even the reflection of the golden rays off the water did little to appease her mind.

"Stay put," Wade repeated as he pushed open the door.

"I was thinking I might go give the murderer-rapist a hug," Artemis said, shaking her head.

Forester wrinkled his nose. "You might… might wanna get down. Just in case."

She noticed the way he was unstrapping his weapon. She let out a faint puff of air, feeling a slow jolt of nerves. She'd come because she wanted to help.

But now, staring at a lakeside home, with a panoramic view, she couldn't think of anything to add. Mostly, she wanted to get a look at JB himself. Perhaps he'd be able to shed some light on the postcards.

Wade unsnapped his holster too. Both men were shooting each other looks over the top of the car. Artemis decided perhaps it was best to take their advice.

Slowly, she lowered her head, ducking behind the seats and reclining—almost lying down—across the back row. She continued studying the phone, frowning as she did.

Forester gave a quick, "Looking good." Then slammed the door. Wade followed.

She wasn't sure if Forester's comment had been harmless approval of her protective posture or something more obnoxious. Artemis still hadn't had a chance to reprimand Forester about his earlier comments, but the sheer cheek of the man was beginning to rub her the wrong way.

Normally, comments like that were reserved for fans of her streaming site or chess aficionados in the forums.

She shook her head, muttering darkly, preferring the puzzle in her hand to the one now moving towards the two-story lake home.

Another postcard. This one had a picture of an elk in the woods.

She frowned now. What if the pictures corresponded to the strange letters? What if one postcard's text applied to *another's* pictures. With this in mind, she began scanning again.

She heard voices now. A sudden *bang.* Then shouting. The sound of a slamming door. "FBI! FBI!"

Artemis glanced briefly over the edge of the seat.

No gunshots for the moment.

At least that was good.

She sighed. Part of her was now wondering something else.

Not just what her father wanted from Joseph Baker... But what did the recently released man want from the Ghostkiller?

More instruction? Another murder-mentee, perhaps?

She frowned.

And then a window shattered.

She yelped, staring up at the second floor of the house. What looked like a table leg was sticking out from the window above the garage. Forester and Wade had disappeared through the front door now. But an *actual* leg followed the table appendage. Straight through the window, onto the roof of the attached garage.

A large man with a big belly strained as he pulled through the window, muttering, cursing. His face red. He was wearing sweatpants and no shirt. He hit the black roofing, cursed, and tumbled. She watched in horror as the man rolled off the edge of the roof and then hit the ground with a loud yelp.

She wanted to shout for Forester. But suddenly, she realized, she was sitting alone in a car. Forester and Wade were on the *other* side of murder-Santa.

Mr. Baker was groaning as he pushed to his feet, trying to keep quiet though. His big, bushy, white beard had a few strands of glass from his foray through the second-floor window.

Now, though, he stumbled forward, hastening towards the road while tugging at his sweatpants and limping.

As he moved, the big man cursed and gasped, his cheeks red, face sweaty. Clearly, his fall from the roof had injured his leg.

"Hey!" Forester's voice. The agent was now looking through the window. Wade was sprinting out of the front door, weapon raised.

Joseph Baker cursed, glancing around, and then—still holding his wooden table leg like a club—he rushed towards the parked FBI vehicle.

Artemis' eyes widened.

And she remembered her last trip into Seattle with Forester.

At the time...

He'd left the keys in the ignition.

She looked sharply between the seats, eyes past the steering wheel towards—

Shit.

A small fob dangled from the ignition. She cursed, trying to sit upright, to reach towards the keys, but Mr. Baker was already at the front door.

He hadn't seen her yet, judging by his hunched form trying to take cover from Forester's angle, and his quick glances towards Wade.

The two FBI agents were now racing out of the house, shouting, weapons raised. But they didn't fire.

Artemis was in the car. She realized neither of them wanted to hit her.

Dammit. Split-second, she ducked in the backseat, deciding there was no time to reach the keys. Just as she darted out of sight, she heard a loud *smash.*

The front window went the same way as the second-story one. A large wooden table leg cleared the window hastily. Wade was shouting. Forester yelled, "FBI! STOP!"

"Yeah right," Baker muttered beneath his breath.

At least, Artemis decided, he hadn't realized the door was already open. The smashed window had been unnecessary.

Baker pulled the door handle on the inside, swinging it open. He slid with a grunt and a straining sound into the front seat. Still no gunshots. He glanced at the keys, chuckling now. "Idiots," he muttered breathlessly.

He smelled of beer and beef jerky.

He twisted the keys. The engine purred to life. A newer model—no hesitation. As if the car itself were attempting to aid Baker in his escape.

Artemis hunched in the back seat, terror flooding her system. Tentatively, she reached for the door handle, breathing in shallow puffs. Maybe, if she timed it right, she could get out of the car before he could stop her.

Maybe if...

The car began to reverse, and as it did, two red-ringed eyes looked back through the rear window, stuttering lips cursing and huffing as they—

The eyes landed on her.

Widened.

She stared back. Squeaked. She reached desperately for the door handle.

His meaty palm slammed the locks on the front door.

9

She tried to pull the lock; Baker hollered at her, yelling and reaching for her wrist desperately. Panic, terror flooded her system. He grabbed her wrist, yanking it down, but the motion caused the car to nearly swerve off the road.

Artemis screamed now.

"Shut up!" he hissed at her. He swerved the other way, trying to reverse down the driveway while gripping her wrist. He'd dropped his wooden table leg now, and it rested on the passenger seat in the front. Artemis yanked desperately, but he was picking up speed, faster, faster.

The FBI agents couldn't risk shooting because she was in the car.

But now, her terror had reached new levels. Her skin crawled, her breath came in rapid gasps. She could feel a panic attack coming.

"No, no, no," she muttered in a moan. Not now. *Not now!*

One enemy at a time. That was what Helen had often told her when they'd been growing up. A lot of the little lessons Helen had imparted to her younger sister still stuck around to this day.

But as Artemis jounced and jerked, rolling in the back seat with the erratic motions of the vehicle, her heart kept pounding horribly. She was hyperventilating. The FBI didn't have another vehicle. She wondered if the local police would even respond to a call if they knew *she* was the one in danger.

Focus. She had to focus.

"Hand-delivered," Baker was muttering. "Gave me a car, a broad. Gonna have to express my gratitude to the feds." He chortled now, his red face turned back towards the road as he veered out of the long driveway, beneath the trees, and turned onto the lakeside road.

The tires squealed.

Artemis had to think. She glanced again, eyes wide, desperate, fixating on the wooden club in the front seat.

But no... no she couldn't overpower Baker. He was far larger than her. Far stronger, judging by his grip which he still hadn't relaxed, one arm dangling back, holding her in place.

She knew someone like Forester might have just broken the arm.

She eyed where the shoulder jutted past the seat, extending back towards her. But this also seemed risky. *Think... Think...*

And then it struck her.

Not a Forester move. An Artemis one.

She wasn't the aggressive opener Helen had always been. She preferred to play the opponent. And she knew a few things about *this* particular opponent.

And so, though a panic-attack had half arisen in her chest and though she wanted little more than to scream, Artemis used one of the breathing tricks she'd been taught by the stable of psychologists and counselors she'd worked her way through—mostly without success—over the years.

In for five seconds, out for seven. Slow... calm... even in the horrifying situation, her heart racing, her skin prickling, she at least was able to slow her breathing. It felt as if fingers were attempting to squeeze her lungs.

But now, she tried to channel her inner Grant, forcing out stern, harsh words.

"My father won't be pleased to hear you wanted to hurt me! He sent me to help you."

It was a lie. A bold lie—a clear bluff, but grounded in a devastating truth. Joseph Baker had been corresponding with the Ghostkiller ever since he'd been released from prison.

The man glanced in the mirror, smirking, his lips curling—occasionally his eyes would glaze with panic when he glanced in the rearview mirror—but when he spotted no one in pursuit, he returned to the business of leering.

"Want me to be your daddy, hun?" he said, adding another chuckle.

"I'm not sure what Otto would think of that," she replied, her voice steely despite the shivers of revulsion down her spine.

The name did it.

The moment she said it, he stiffened. He glanced in the rearview mirror, but this time adjusting it to get a good look at her. She glared back, her mismatched eyes staring into the reflective glass.

And suddenly, he released her wrist as if he'd been scalded. He nearly veered off the road, tires squealing as he swerved.

"I..." he swallowed. "Shit. I—so... Artemis? Artemis, right? I remember you. Holy shit. You're... my God." He was stuttering, sweaty, his face red again. Now, his eyes bugged in a sort of panic that hadn't been displayed even while being chased by gun-toting FBI agents.

Artemis kept her expression rigid, projecting far, far more confidence than she felt. Sitting in the backseat of a stolen car, facing a suspected serial killer, her skin continued to prickle. Her stomach continued to protest and twist.

She wanted to vomit, but any show of fear would break the spell.

Men like this *enjoyed* fear. They thirsted at the scent of it.

And so she kept her glare affixed, her eyes never leaving the gaze in the rearview mirror. She gave the faintest shakes of her head. She kept her voice low, in control, wondering if he could hear the tremor existing just on the fringes. "Now," she said, quietly, "explain yourself. I wonder what my father will think when he hears how you treated me."

The man was gaping, bug-eyed into the mirror. He kept muttering quick protests. She thought of all the postcards addressed to her father in prison. Of all the effort this man had gone through to stay connected.

"He won't hurt them, will he?" whispered the large man. "I did everything he asked."

Artemis stared, her pulse pounding. She couldn't reveal that she didn't have a clue what he was talking about. The atmosphere had shifted, though. Clearly her bluff was paying off.

Her father clearly had his hooks in this man.

"He put you up to it?" she murmured.

The man nodded adamantly. "Y-yes! Of course he did! And let me tell you, those damn postcards were a hell of a hassle."

She nodded slowly, sitting upright now, leaning back and crossing her arms in a show of ease she certainly didn't feel. "So, Mr. Baker," she murmured, "What am I to do with you?" More power posturing. Simple, straightforward.

He hesitated, but then suddenly, his eyes narrowed, and he glared. "Hang on—what if you're a Fed?" he said suddenly. His nose wrinkled. "Shit—you are, aren't you? This is a dupe! I'm not an idiot!" he began to scream, spittle flying and flecking the dashboard. His meaty fists gripped the steering wheel, but one dislodged to reach for his wooden club.

Artemis had to think fast, her mind whirring. She said the first thing she could think of. "If I were a dupe, would I know about your pill problem? Or what about the nightmares you've been having? Hmm? The ones that keep you up at night—the terrifying dreams... Is that something a dupe would know?"

He calmed again, staring into the mirror as if he'd seen a ghost. "You... you're psychic too?"

He's not psychic. She wanted to scream. But instead, she just nodded. "Yes... just like my father, who sent me."

"How did you... how could you?"

Red-ringed eyes from sleep deprivation. No yawning, though, suggesting physiological acclimation to a long-term sleep issue. A criminal history, years spent in prison seeing horrible things. Guessing at nightmares as the source of insomnia wasn't a stretch. Apnea was another option, but she'd flipped the coin. Besides, one nasty, little thing about rapists and serial killers was their affinity for *fear*. Fear could be external, due to childhood trauma, or conjured by the imagination. As far as she'd been able to tell, Mr. Baker lived *alone* in his lakehouse. In a beautiful, scenic location. Not external then. So if imagination or trauma, the fear then was likely to manifest in more than just dreams.

But this was the trick with proper charlatans. Finding a *general* realization but addressing something specific as if it were an impressive discovery. For instance, all men Mr. Baker's age and size were on *some* sort of heart medication or similar. But a trickster, a mentalist would *narrow* the observation.

She could just have easily had said something about, *the last argument with your doctor.*

It was the same observation, but the man's personality and inevitable interaction with a primary care physician suggested conflict of *some* sort was inevitable. The trick was never narrowing too much or being *too* specific.

There was a trick with an invisible string she'd once seen her father pull on stage. He had simple, invisible thread—purchasable for a couple of bucks from any hack magician's store. But he spread it between his fingers and invited two guests on stage. He would waft his fingers over their faces. To the audience, it looked as if he wasn't touching them at all. But Artemis knew the invisible thread was scraping their noses.

After having them close their eyes and telling them *not* to open them, her father would move his fingers over their faces slowly. He wouldn't say anything. Within the *first* ten seconds, he would scrape the nose of one of the audience members with the thread.

And then, after another few seconds, he'd walk over to the second audience member. He would say something like, "Sometimes, our mental connections are stronger than you think!" And then he'd point to the rest of the audience, making sure they were watching. He would go about some flashy hand motions, some ridiculous preamble.

All of it was to help the audience to forget how he had moved his hand over the face of the first person in the first few seconds.

Once this was forgotten, he would turn to the second person, who he was now standing next to. The two audience volunteers would be facing each other across a ten-foot gap in the stage, but they kept their eyes obediently sealed.

Then, he would visibly *touch* the nose of the second volunteer with his finger, usually an attractive woman to further distract.

The process was simple. Move a hand near the face *without* touching the first woman. Help the audience forget. Move to the second woman, and nearly a minute later, touch her nose.

And only then would he shout, loudly to the *first* woman. "Be honest! Did you feel anything."

Of course, her eyes had been closed. She didn't realize the *audience* was assuming he meant in the last few seconds. Whereas in her mind, she was recalling when the invisible thread had scraped her nose a minute ago.

So she would nod.

The audience would gasp.

Then, with an urgent, self-important tone, her father would declare, "Tell them! Tell them where you felt it!" He would still often be touching the second woman's nose.

The first woman would hesitate and point to her own nose.

The audience would erupt. The mentalist would lower his hands and hastily step back between the two women.

And by the time they opened their eyes, neither woman realized they'd *both* been lied to. The invisible thread trick had bamboozled *many* people. It was all in the assumptions, in narrowing the focus and redirecting *the when* of the reveal. Timing mattered. The women were lied to. The audience lied to.

Only a person who knew about the invisible thread and paid close attention to the first few seconds would notice *anything*.

It was all quite clever, and hard to track for someone inexperienced in such tricks.

But Artemis had grown up around it. Had trained with her father. And now, even more importantly, had trained in strategy and tactics for most of her adult life.

She hated it, but she was channeling her father's facial expressions. Self-important, grandiosity. Chin tilted, eyes only *faintly* narrowed. Shoulders thrown back; she'd even added the faint, airy whisper quality to her words.

And now Joseph Baker was staring at her in absolute awe. He let out a faint little mewling sound. "The dreams," he whispered. "Please... can you make them stop, too?"

Artemis didn't understand this part. But she knew when she had a willing mind. She said, firmly, "I'll help, but you need to drive back to your house *right now.*"

He stared at her, wrinkling his nose. "There's cops back there," he said.

Artemis let out a quick huff of air. "They'll be gone."

"H-how do you know?"

She tilted her head, allowing him to fill in the blanks.

"Oh... oh shit... You're sure?" he said, still moaning.

"Do you want me to save you from those dreams?" she whispered back, her voice still airy, still spewing lies. She didn't *like* doing it, but she also knew that if she allowed Baker to escape the police, other women might die.

Plus, she very much wanted to be *out* of this car.

She held his gaze in the mirror, wondering what her father might do. She needed an extra inch of authority. Of gravitas. And so she said the one thing that she knew would help. "I know about the postcards," she said simply. "My father told me everything. How would that be possible otherwise? Now turn around, please. Head back."

Of course, she didn't know *anything* about the postcards, except that they existed.

But Mr. Baker now seemed sufficiently convinced he could trust her.

Or, perhaps, more accurately, *fear* her.

Secondhand fear wasn't nearly as strong as firsthand terror. But in that moment, it did help turn the car around. Baker was muttering to himself, one eye twitching nervously. The red coloring of his cheeks had faded to sheet-white.

Artemis murmured, "What's worse, Joseph? Crossing the FBI? Or crossing my father. He wants you to go back. You'd better listen."

"He... he wants me to? How do you know?"

She tapped her forehead, raising her eyebrows. "I'm speaking to him right now," she said. "He wants to thank you. He says to call you... JB."

She felt ridiculous. Now, she was scraping the bottom of the barrel for *anything* that might give her some credence.

But it seemed to work.

"I—I'm not trying to make him mad," Baker whispered. "I've been helping. I keep helping."

"Yes, and now how you must help is to go back."

Baker sighed, blinking sleepily in the rearview mirror. He shook his head in some confusion, but then, with a heavy air of resignation, he floored the gas, hastening *back* in the direction of his lakeside home.

10

CAMERON FORESTER COULD FEEL his temper rising. He was barking instructions into his phone. Now, three other police cars tore into the driveway.

Backup.

Late as ever.

He glared at the local cops who were pushing out of their vehicles, their expressions wreathed in the flashing red and blue lights of their vehicles.

He wanted to pause and give the tardy men and women in their beige uniforms something of a tongue-lashing.

But none of that would help Artemis.

He growled now, marching up the driveway, his long legs taking him back beneath the jutting, black roof of the garage. His feet kicked particles of glass, sending them scattering.

He shot a look up, scowling towards the smashed window. He'd been too eager. He never should have let Artemis come with them. It was so hard to keep track of all the *little* things. Forester thought of himself as a big-picture type of guy.

He watched as some of the cops were now approaching hastily. Agent Wade stood in the front of the house, arms crossed, barking instructions. Already, they'd made enough phone calls to block half the roads in the county.

Forester's voice was hoarse from shouting over his radio.

For a moment, he wondered if it might be worth stealing one of the cops' cars and going for a chase himself. But Joseph Baker already had a twenty-minute head start. No... no better to trust the APB and to coordinate for the moment.

Maybe they'd find something useful in the damn lakeside home.

Forester could feel his fingers curling, his knuckles tense. He wanted to scream now. To kick pinecones and pine needles. But while he hadn't *always* been good at controlling his more violent tendencies... he'd improved in recent years. He'd picked up fighting in his youth—it had been the one avenue for his aggression at the time.

He liked to think of himself as a sociopath with self-control. For instance, he'd wanted to lurch across that interview table and wring the neck of Otto Blythe.

But he'd held himself back. With some help from the others.

He glanced towards the driveway where they'd parked their car.

"Dammit," he muttered beneath his breath, emitting an incoherent sound as he ran his hand over his face, groaning as he did. "How stupid..."

Wade was issuing quick instructions for the search pattern they were forming. Roadblocks were set up, but a few of the smaller roads around the lake would need to be manually searched. More backup was on its way.

As he began to move hastily again towards Wade, frowning at the thought of Artemis in that back seat, Forester took a brief pause, mid-step—lowering his radio—to try and *think* through his emotions.

That's what the psych-eval lady had told him. Grant, of course, had already guaranteed he'd pass. But the FBI shrink had told Forester that *thinking* emotions was a useful tool for someone like him. His mind didn't often form the same emotional connections others did.

He didn't cry. Didn't feel fear. The affections he felt were often only glimmers unless he *consciously* and carefully went out of his way to nurture them.

He liked Artemis Blythe. He wasn't fond of her. Emotions hadn't taken root. But she was attractive, smart, *useful.* Three things he greatly valued.

Plus... she had a sense of humor. This more than anything deserved some type of accolade. He could still picture the look on her face when he'd waved her down at her chess tournament. He smirked, considering the way some of the crowd had reacted.

He stretched his long frame, arms over his head as Wade issued the final set of instructions. Now, the search party would move out rapidly, tightening the noose around the lake. Forester tried to *think* what the appropriate emotional response might be in this moment.

Fight or flight were his realm of expertise. Everything that came before or after was mostly just a headache.

But... fear. Perhaps. Concern, certainly. He felt *some* concern. He noted this emotion, trying to focus on it, to allow it to lift in his consciousness.

Just because his mind didn't make the same emotional connections as others' did, didn't mean he couldn't be a good man.

He'd often wondered as a child *why* he should be a good man. He didn't have the same emotional pay-off rewarding him for *feeling* good.

But that had all changed seven years ago.

Forester scowled as he stomped down the driveway once more towards where Wade was waving him over.

Seven years ago... then three years ago. Two landmark moments. Everything had changed, but no one had been there. Not in deep Louisiana, amidst a swamp, on an airboat under the blistering sun. No one could have known a thing.

So how did the damn Ghostkiller know. Forester had seen it in the man's eyes. He *knew*. Somehow—some way, Artemis' father had found out what had happened. Not even Agent Grant knew. No one did. And if anyone found out...

Forester felt a spike of *some* emotion... he couldn't quite identify this one.

He'd wanted to punch Otto Blythe, and now he was beginning to regret he hadn't. The man was psychic, wasn't he?

Artemis claimed there were no such things. But Forester had seen far, far too much. Down in Louisiana, in that swampy marsh, amidst those who claimed voodoo, claimed other, darker things... He'd *seen* things. At least, he thought he had.

The Ghostkiller wasn't a normal man. Wasn't *good* at all.

Forester tried his best to do the right thing even without the usual dopamine reward system. But he recognized evil when he saw it. He'd joined the FBI because of this very recognition.

"Alright, you coming with me or searching the house?" Wade was saying as Forester finally approached.

The air was tense. Nearly eight law enforcement officers were beginning to scatter, off to fulfill their given instructions.

Forester frowned, his expression grim.

"Probably best if... I..." He trailed off, slowly. He stared.

"Forester?" Wade said. "Are you—"

But he went quiet suddenly, following Cameron's stare.

The two men watched, mouths slightly open, eyes wide, as their stolen sedan slowly trundled back down the driveway. The front window was open, and through it came the sound of weeping. The sound of a grown man bawling his heart out.

"Is that..." Wade muttered.

Forester resisted the urge to rub his eyes, but he did blink a couple of times just to be sure he wasn't hallucinating.

He caught a sobbing voice say, "...if this is what he wants, okay! Okay!" And then the front door flung open.

Joseph Baker, in all his evil Santa Claus glory, white beard bristling across his ample chest, stumbled from the vehicle.

A second later, the back door clicked, and a slim, dark-haired figure stepped out. A very pale woman with mismatched eyes dusted herself off primly and let out a faint sigh which it looked as if she'd been holding.

Joseph Baker's hands rose into the air, tears streaming down his face to mingle with his pale facial hair.

"Holy shit," Wade muttered. "What the hell?"

Forester just gaped. He swallowed, then said, "Told you she was psychic."

Then, as if a spell was broken, police all seemed to recognize Baker at once. Voices shouted. Boots hit the leaves. Guns left holsters and more than one set of handcuffs were procured. Figures hastened forward, shouting.

"Down on the ground! Get down!"

Forester and Wade shared another stunned look, then both broke into a sprint.

11

Artemis sat across the table from Mr. Baker.

She tried her best to project the same confidence she had summoned back in his getaway car, but this was difficult, given how rapidly her foot was tapping a tattoo into the floor. Agent Wade, who was standing by the door, had objected to having her in the room with them. But Forester had pointed out that Artemis was the one who brought them their suspect. Artemis hadn't been given a vote.

Mostly, she just wanted this nightmare to be over with.

Her fingers rubbed against the fabric of her pocket, feeling the rigid outline of her phone.

She'd received a text message from her brother. Nothing more than a thumbs up.

Whatever the hell that meant. She hadn't texted him... he wasn't responding to anything. Just sending her an emoji finger.

She scowled at the reflective metal surface of the table beneath the bright, fluorescent tube light. Now, they had driven half an hour out of Pinelake in order to borrow the interrogation room of a small sheriff's office where half the force didn't want to see Artemis dead.

Things continued to escalate with the Dawkins family.

Artemis had received another text message from an anonymous number.

This one had simply said, *you won't get away with it*. And then it had included an emoticon of a gun.

She hadn't realized they even made emoticons of firearms.

Now, she wanted nothing more than to solve the case, then have her father sent into solitary confinement where he couldn't talk to another soul.

Joseph Baker sat across the table, fidgeting. The big man with the bushy beard didn't look so much like Santa under the bright lights. The sweat along his forehead and his fidgeting, nervous disposition made him look more like a schoolchild in the principal's office.

If she hadn't seen his rap sheet, she might have felt a little more pity.

He kept glancing at her, hesitating, frowning, wrinkling his nose and opening his mouth as if to speak but then trailing off and shaking his head.

She had told him, before they'd pulled back into the driveway, that her father's plan was to plant her with the FBI. He was helping make that happen.

She wasn't sure if he was nearly as convinced now. But at least they had him handcuffed to the table.

"Mr. Baker," Forester said in a lackadaisical manner. "I do have to say, I'm glad you returned the car."

Wade nodded in agreement, his stony countenance fixed on their suspect.

Forester was sitting in the chair next to Artemis. Wade, leaning by the door, acted like some sort of sentry, watching over the room, his arms crossed over his impressive musculature.

"I don't know what you think I did," said the man with the white beard. Again, his eyes slipped towards Artemis, as if looking for some sort of cue.

She had no clue what to say. Her foot continued to tap nervously. Her fingers continued to trace the outline of her phone, her skin rubbing against the smooth fabric of her trousers. She purchased most of her clothes online, and so it was something of a marvel when she got something that fit perfectly and also didn't feel as if it were made of burlap.

"How about we start with why you ran," Forester said, conversationally. He was leaning back again, in an easy-going posture, his arms not crossed but clasped behind his head as if he were at the beach getting some sun.

"I ran because you broke down my door," said Baker nervously. A thin bead of sweat was trembling at the edge of his lip. His tongue darted out, licking it, and swallowing.

Artemis felt her stomach turn.

"It's all right," she said, slowly, "you can tell them the truth."

She wasn't sure if she could make this work. She also didn't think that she'd kept much goodwill with Baker, having initially promised that no one would be waiting for him back at his house and then subsequently threatening him with her father if he didn't turn himself in.

The man was sleep deprived, dangerous. He believed in psychics and was clearly under her father's thumb.

But he wasn't stupid. At least, not *very* stupid.

And now, as he kept glancing in her direction, she could see some of the charm wearing off.

Even the most strident of believers in the things her father pretended to be had their limit where self-preservation was concerned.

He said, "Y-you want me to tell him?"

Wade was scowling from the door. Artemis just nodded. "It's what my father would want. Tell them everything."

She resisted the urge to wince. She was laying it on a little thick.

"I could," he said in a shaky, hoarse voice. His forearms had left stains of condensation on the metal table. His shirt was also stained with sweat. Patches by the arms and near the neck. She could hear him breathing, a heavy, wheezing sound.

She could see the way his eyes were bloodshot, exhausted.

She said, "Wouldn't it be nice to get it off your chest? You'd finally be able to sleep."

"You want me to tell everything?" He shifted uncomfortably. "I don't know. I thought your dad said not to mention any of it to anyone."

Forester looked irritated now. He said, "Baker, we know what you did. We found Robin."

The large man glanced at Forester.

Artemis leaned in. In as soothing a tone as she could fake, she said, "Just tell them. Tell them everything. Tell them how my father put you up to it."

Baker swallowed, shivering slightly, and then, he said, quietly, "What was your sister's name?"

Artemis blinked in surprise. Forester tensed. Wade was glancing sharply in Artemis' direction.

"I don't see how that's relevant," Artemis said.

But Joseph Baker was shaking his head, snapping his fingers now. *Click. Click.* "No, no, I think I remember now... it was... Helen."

And the moment he said the word, it was as if a button had been pushed.

As if suddenly, like a marionette dangling over a stage, he was animated. A trigger-word... the sort she'd seen before.

Joseph Baker perked up. He sat straight in his seat, smiling all of a sudden. If anything, the unease in his posture, his movements, seemed to fade. He leaned back in the chair, and a slow smile spread from his lips and added a twinkle to his eyes, allowing his shoulders to press back. He went suddenly still.

No more twitching, no more anxious or nervous glances. No more quick lick of the lips like some reptile. No more tapping of fingers together, or rattling of handcuffs. No more shifting of forearms against a sweat-slicked table.

Now, he went still. Like a tombstone. His eyes, like open graves, leered across the table.

"Helen," he repeated. "Your father mentioned her to me," he said quietly.

Forester and Wade were both tense. Artemis, though, wasn't nearly as surprised. She had seen the effect of hypnosis on willing minds before. Hypnosis was not, as many suspected, a supernatural phenomenon. Rather, it was a psychological one.

It depended on the subject, the willingness, and the activator. This had always been one of her father's least favorite tricks. Also, the least predictable. In her experience, hypnotism, during her father's shows, had a ninety percent failure rate.

Mostly, it was placebo. Primarily, it was suggestion.

The strongest suggestions could often be triggered by a word.

And in this case, that word was clear.

Helen.

Artemis felt prickles along her neck, and her eyes narrowed.

"I don't care what my father mentioned to you," Artemis said quietly. "Tell us about Robin Dawkins. Why did you kill her?"

This time, Baker didn't look anything besides confused.

"Kill?" He snorted. "What are you talking about?" The big man shook his head. "You don't know what's going on here, do you? You don't know anything about the postcards. Otto said you might come asking questions. He said if you mentioned Helen, I should tell you something."

Artemis shivered. Forester was leaning forward, as if ready to intervene at a moment's notice.

"Tell me what?"

"Do you really want to know?"

He was speaking words in a tone that didn't match his earlier one. Words, through persuasion, suggestion, through the weakness of his mind, that he had allowed her own father to plant. And yet words she wanted to hear.

"Tell me," she said firmly. Her foot was no longer tapping. Like Baker, she went very still.

"Helen is alive," he said simply.

And the moment he said it, the spell broke. He blinked a few times, as if rousing from a trance, and then began glancing around the table, scowling at anyone who met his gaze.

Artemis wanted to yell. What was her father playing at?

He'd given her the same message, through another one of his lackeys the previous week. Erik Kramer had told her the same thing. It was why she had visited him in prison.

What did her father gain by convincing Artemis that her sister was alive?

She thought back to what her father had said in prison. The man who had kidnapped Helen was the real Ghostkiller. But she didn't believe it. Didn't believe *him*.

If Helen was alive, what were the chances she had survived some form of captivity for more than seventeen years?

Helen had been five years older than Artemis and would have spent nearly two decades trapped in some horrible prison.

The idea that her sister still lived was almost as horrifying as the death Artemis had come to terms with.

"Tell us about Robin Dawkins," Forester snapped, guiding them back on track.

But now, the man was shaking his head. "The sheriff's granddaughter?"

"So you know her," said Wade from the door.

"Everyone knows everyone around these parts. I had to move homes twice just to avoid harassment. I'm now on the far side of the lake, and people still don't leave me alone. People like you." He was twitching nervously again, but also seemed genuinely angry. "I've paid my debt," he snapped. "It isn't right that you keep harassing me!"

Forester scowled. "You were serving a life sentence that got commuted because of a crooked cop. You didn't pay anything."

Baker returned the glare. "I'm a free man. You have no right. I'm going to sue you!"

Artemis was watching the show, confused. She glanced between Forester and Wade. Her eyes moved to their suspect. Sitting there, now, considering her options, she realized it didn't make sense.

According to the coroner, someone had chased Robin through the woods. Robin had been a runner, an athlete. This man wouldn't have been able to catch her.

So why had he fled the FBI?

"Tell us about the postcards," she interjected. She knew Wade didn't like it when she spoke during interrogations. He hadn't even wanted her in the room, but if she was going to be a consultant, then she would damn well *consult*!

"What postcards?"

"That's why you ran," she said.

"I sure as hell didn't kill anyone," he repeated.

"You were convicted of murder," Forester pointed out.

Baker snapped, "Again. I didn't kill anyone, *again*."

"Hard for me to believe that," Forester snapped back. "Your house is right across the lake from where Robin was killed."

"It's a big lake, dude. *Lake* is in the name of the town. That's not evidence, it's wishful thinking."

Forester was scowling now. "Where were you this morning?"

"At the post office," he retorted. And then he caught himself, and said, a bit calmer, "In town. Just doing errands. It wasn't a big thing."

Wade was now approaching the table. "So why did you run?"

"You keep asking that. I thought you were home invaders."

"Do better than that," Forester retorted. "We announced ourselves."

"I'm dyslexic. Didn't help you shouting jumbled letters."

"You stole my car."

"I thought it was mine."

"That's how you want to play this, then?"

"I'm not playing at all. You're the one playing games with my life. I did *not* kill that girl. I didn't even hear about it until I saw it on the news."

"It was on the news?" Artemis cut in quickly. She remembered the news van and camera crew trying to get past the police blockade back at the barn. She pressed her teeth tightly in frustration, wondering if her image was now being displayed across the internet for the entire chess community to see. Being seen anywhere *near* this case would bring more baggage than she wanted.

But the men ignored her. Artemis frowned. Normally, the Dawkins family was good at suppressing any stories that might detrimentally hurt their family. But she supposed that if they were hoping to rile the town against her, they might release certain information to the public. She wondered what exactly the news bulletin said. She doubted it was very flattering where she was concerned.

"So you were sending a postcard," Forest insisted. "Got proof of that?"

The big man looked Forester directly in the eyes. His smirk had returned. This wasn't the confident grin of someone living out emotions given to a malleable mind but the smirk of a scumbag who knew he had the upper hand. "Security footage," he said with a grin. "Post offices have cameras. Look at them. I was there all morning, sending... well, *stuff*."

"Let me guess, more postcards?"

"No law against keeping in touch with old friends," he replied.

Forester and Wade both glanced to Artemis now. She felt like a deer in the headlights. She swallowed hesitantly, shifted uncomfortably. Her foot was once again tapping in rhythm against the concrete. She knew they wanted her to say something on the postcards front. That was why he had run. He was too big. She believed that the alibi would check out. She believed that he was at least telling the truth about Robin.

Her father was playing with them again. But it almost felt like there were two threats at once. Something with these postcards and then the murder.

But she still had no clue what the postcards meant. She sighed and shot a look towards Forester, "It might be worth checking that footage from the post office."

Joseph Baker leaned back with a satisfied smirk. Forester pushed out of his chair in a huff. Wade watched it all, like an old, stone gargoyle perched on the edge of a building. Artemis simply felt miserable.

Her father, somehow, had anticipated she would speak with Joseph Baker. Two years ago.

The only way he could have planted subliminal messaging would have been in person. When Baker had still been in prison.

Two years ago, her father had anticipated this moment. Or at least one like it.

What other traps, ambushes, and tricks were out there. How long had he been preparing?

What was he preparing for?

What was the code in the postcards?

Artemis could feel the sense of frustration over the room. The two FBI agents were now conferring in the dark beneath the doorway, murmuring quietly. Artemis refused to look in the direction of Baker. She pushed out of her seat. The metal chair legs scraped against the ground.

She grimaced at the sound but turned, moving slowly back towards the door.

She believed Baker. He was too big to chase a girl down in the woods. Her father was involved but not killing by proxy. At least, not with Baker.

But he was the only person who her father had been friendly with in that prison that was currently out.

She frowned, shaking her head, trying desperately to think through her options.

Forester was raising his voice as he spoke urgently with Wade.

But she didn't listen. Grant had insisted she stay. But what if...

Surely they knew Artemis had nothing to do with it. What if she just slipped away? Took a taxi, went back to California?

She could spend the trip analyzing some games with the Washingtons over the Internet.

That would be far nicer than this current debacle.

Then again, while a ride back home would be nice, who would stop her father?

Who would intervene?

Ten women would die. That's what he had said. He had known where the first body would be.

But how?

She dipped her head as she reached the doorway and the arguing FBI agents. She rubbed her temples.

She couldn't leave yet. As much as she wanted to, she couldn't just slip away.

People were counting on her.

Lives were on the line.

12

THE WOODSMAN SHIVERED HORRIBLY, his knees crowded against his chest in the metal tub. The freezing, ice-cold water lapped against his goose-bump covered skin. Small pieces of ice bumped against him, swirling around him, and he ducked his head back into the liquid again.

And he started to count.

Slowly, painstakingly.

One... two... three...

It was equal parts peaceful and terrifying down here. The memories simply didn't go away. So cold. So scared. Shaking and trying to scream. Needles of frigid material piercing his lungs. A scream caught in his chest.

As he kept his head under, in the freezing water of his bathtub, the woodsman began to cry, like he always did.

But even the tears were carried away by the liquid. Tears meant nothing to a lake. Nothing, even, to a bathtub. Tears were only whispers in a room of screaming.

But as a child, he'd cried... *a lot.*

Fifty-five... Fifty-six... Fifty-seven...

Now, he could feel his lungs protesting. Could feel his mind threatening to frighten him. But it was on the other side of terror where peace was claimed.

Pain was nothing. Pain was a friend.

He'd trained with Navy SEALs, hadn't he? BUDS—the school for the SEALs. The dropout rate, last he'd heard, was nearly eighty percent.

Eighty percent of the *best* in the military failed to pass.

He could remember the embarrassing little ding-a-ling of the bell whenever one of the recruits quit.

But he hadn't quit. In fact, he'd passed *twice.* The first time, he'd been bounced for an injury to his leg. The second...

The second he'd failed on psych-eval. Honorably discharged.

If there was such a thing.

Things had gone sideways after that. They'd trained him to be a killing machine. Then shown him the door with a quick *thanksomuch, haveanicelife.*

But there was nothing nice about his life.

The last girl had found out the hard way... He drowned her... Brought her back...

Then drowned her again... Four times she'd drowned before she'd finally given in. It had taken him a couple of hours. And then the business with the kayak.

Two minutes fifteen. Two minutes sixteen. Two minutes seventeen.

Dark spots were now threatening his eyes. One of the training regimens in the SEAL school had been a drowning practice. It happened far more than the media was ever told. Five times in the same year, the instructors had taken him and the rest of the class to a swimming pool. Five times they'd dropped him in the deep end and forced him to the bottom of the pool.

If someone tapped out in that moment, the team *knew* they'd never cut it.

And so the instructors helped drown them.

Five times they'd drowned him.

But the terror had possessed him each time. After what had happened all those years ago. What *she* had done to him.

He snarled now, the last of his air lost through curled lips, fleeing to the surface as bubbles.

Three minutes one second. Three minutes two.

He was nearly unconscious now. Sometimes... *rare* occasions... he wondered what would happen if he just went the full way.

Few humans had enough willpower to drown themselves.

He knew he could do it. He'd done it before, under the watch of Navy instructors.

But now... now he had other business to attend to.

He surged from the frigid, ice bath, gasping deeply as his head broke the surface and he emerged in light. A faint, flickering flame sparked from the fireplace in the far corner of the small cabin. He gasped, water dripping down his face, tapping against the surface of the bathtub.

Inhale, exhale... More than three minutes. Not great. Not great at all.

But still... enough.

Enough for a head start at least.

"Three..." he gasped. "Minutes..." he said. "You'd better run."

He blinked, looking up now, and staring at the woman dangling from the rafters of the small cabin.

Her eyes stared at him with panic. They often were scared of him. He was... *large.* According to some. The woman's hands were tied above her head. She wore a sheer, white outfit he'd dressed her in. The rest of her clothing was now feeding the fire.

The young woman stared at him, still sobbing, still emitting faint, pathetic sounds.

He hated this part. The crying, the blubbering, the begging.

The ocean didn't take pleading. The lake couldn't hear the sobs. And he, most of all, was indifferent to their pleading.

"P-please," the woman was gasping, wincing every time she shifted, her arms most likely out of joint by now.

He stared at her, shaking his head. "Three minutes," he said simply. He stepped from his brass bathtub, water pouring from him in sheets. He wore no clothing, his massive chest rising and falling as he tried to steady his breathing.

He reached out, snagging a towel from where he'd left it draped over a coat rack. He fixed it to his waist and then snatched a second item—this one from on top of the small, kitchen table. The cabin was only a single room, and because of the length of his arms, he could reach most items with only a couple of steps.

And now, knife in hand, he approached the whimpering woman.

"Only three," he said. "You get a chance. Take it. A storm is coming."

He reached up with the knife. She started kicking, screaming, thrashing.

Fight in her. He smiled at this, nodding. With one massive hand, though, he caught an entire leg and held it as if it were a twig.

"Stop," he growled.

But she didn't. She kept screaming like a banshee. He reached up with his other hand, knife flashing in the firelight.

The rope was cut.

She dropped as he released his grip on her leg.

She hit the floorboards with a gasp, staring in fright at him. She swallowed. "P-please."

"Two minutes, thirty seconds," he said quietly, counting in his head.

"Please!" she said. "I—I can't. What do you want from me? My mother—do you know who she is? She can pay you! Whatever you want."

"Two minutes, twenty seconds," he said, dispassionately. He pointed one large finger towards the open door to his cabin.

"What do you want!" she protested, her voice squeaking.

He looked her directly in the eyes. And then, at the top of his voice, bellowed, "RUN!"

She squeaked and stumbled, scrambling across the floorboards now, shooting panicked glances back towards him. "I—please—"

"RUN!" he screamed again.

And she did. The white, flowing, gossamer cloth fluttering behind her. She ran, stumbling through the open door. Barefoot, onto the leaves, across the detritus.

He wasn't wearing shoes, either, though.

It had to be fair.

Justice... Wasn't that what they all said?

Justice... And so this... this was a drowning man's justice.

He waited a few seconds and then broke into a sprint of his own, hollering after her. "Two minutes! Only two!"

He picked up the pace, surging through his doorway, his wide shoulders barely fitting as they grazed the wood.

13

An air of defeat lingered in the break room.

Artemis and Forester were both frowning at Wade. The laconic agent was shaking his head, and repeating, "I double checked. It's him." His eyes were glued to his screen, studying video footage. "This morning... like he said, at that post office." Wade looked up in disgust. "No way he was at the lake in our time frame."

Forester slapped a hand against the back of a wooden chair by the break room table. He was leaning on a lumpy couch, nursing a Styrofoam cup of coffee, and having partaken in a Tupperware he'd snatched from the fridge with a note that read, *Mavis—don't eat*. The note fluttered past the red, plastic lid as he pillaged the cold enchilada.

Despite his food pilfering ways, Artemis couldn't help but share his sentiment. Instead of slapping chairs, though, she returned her attention to her phone, cycling through the screenshots of the postcards.

The words just didn't make sense. She had been taught to recognize patterns, but there *were* none. If Joseph Baker wasn't their killer, then what was he communicating with her father for? She lowered her phone with a frustrated sigh.

"Yuck, refried beans," Forester muttered, wrinkling his nose and poking at his stolen food.

Artemis shot him a glance. "I'll be sure to tell Mavis to avoid those next time."

Wade was pacing now by the door. "Kayak wasn't rented. Checked everywhere. All kayaks accounted for... He must've brought it with."

"Wire," Forester said, "a damn coat hanger. Sharpened on the end. So no go on that." He sighed. "So what now? What are we missing?" His eyes darted from Artemis to Wade and back. "A sheriff's granddaughter is dead. And we've got nothing. Everything that might have gone wrong for Robin *did.*"

"No witnesses?" Wade asked.

"None."

"What about that pepper spray?"

Artemis frowned. "What pepper spray? Robin had pepper spray?"

Forester shook his head, though. Wade scowled. "In her car—she didn't bring it with her." This was the most agitated she'd seen Desmond Wade. Forester had once quipped that the field office had nicknamed Wade "Ox," and she didn't fault them. The man was built for hauling things.

"Might have to speak with the sergeant," Forester said glumly. "At least, see if he'll talk."

Artemis winced at this suggestion. "You think that's a good idea?"

"I don't have any better. Your father is the one who said this is a serial case... Right now, that's the first thing I'm thinking." Forester lowered his stolen enchilada, frowning as he did. "The longer it takes us, the greater chance we're going to find *another* body."

"What about the jogging trail?" Artemis said. "Has anyone gone back over it?"

Forester nodded. "Yeah. Locals. Gonna be hard to see what they've found though, unless they're in a sharing mood."

Wade was still pacing, scowling as he did.

Forester shot a look at his partner. "What's got you all twisted?"

Wade paused, frowning. "Don't like water," he said simply.

Forester snorted. "Good thing we're in a lake town, then, huh?"

Desmond returned to muttering. Forester waved a hand in Artemis' direction. "Well, psychic. Do your thing. This is where we need you."

"I'm not psychic. There's no such—"

"Don't tell me *that*. Not after meeting your old man." Forester frowned.

Artemis let out a long breath. "It's true—believe it or not. My father is getting information, somehow. That's how he knows about you… About this killer. About the body beneath the dock."

"Right. Getting information," Forester said, swirling a finger near his head.

"Not like that…" Artemis frowned, trying to think through her next step. Mostly, she wanted to hole up in a hotel somewhere and begin preparations for next month's tournament. A lot was still on the line. She could become the first woman to win Nationals. Her sights were set on Worlds. No one had ever broken the 3000-rating barrier before. She was nearly three hundred points shy… A lot of ground to make up.

But she was determined.

She admired Robin for that. Determination looked like waking up early, sticking to a routine.

Artemis was out of her routine, and she hated it. She hesitated, frowning slowly. "I guess… I guess we never voiced it out loud… But the killer was waiting for Robin, right?" She looked over, glancing at Forester and Wade.

They frowned back.

Artemis said. "Robin was a creature of habit. She stuck to her morning runs… what if the killer knew about these? Was waiting for her specifically…"

"Does that help us?" Forester said.

Artemis had perked up now, though, leaning forward and trying to hold back her rising sense of excitement. "It might, actually. Think about it—someone was lying in wait for her. Which meant someone knew her schedule..."

"A lot of people knew Robin's schedule," Forester replied. "She *is* the sheriff's granddaughter. She was popular at school."

"But to know *when* and *where* she would be?" Artemis countered.

"What are you getting at."

Artemis was on her feet now, fingers tapping nervously against her thigh. "I'm thinking... that barring Sergeant Dawkins sharing his own daughter's running schedule with some creep, then what's the best way to know someone's routine?"

"What?" Forester said.

"Observing it. Right? Observing her routine."

"So... so you think she was followed?"

"See—exactly!" Artemis exclaimed, pointing a finger, eyes widening now. "She was a police daughter. Her brothers, her father, her grand-father. Wade said she was required to carry pepper spray with her." Artemis was now drumming her fingers so quickly, she felt as if she'd been the one drinking from Forester's Styrofoam cup of caffeine. "She isn't the type to be followed again and again. The only way to determine a routine is if the killer kept an eye on her more than once. To notice a certain pattern. But like we said, she's from a police family. Follows a routine. She has pepper spray. What are the odds she wouldn't notice a tail?"

Forester wrinkled his nose. "That's a stretch."

But Wade shook his head. "No—she's right. Cop parents are something extra."

Artemis noticed the authority behind this comment. It didn't surprise her that Desmond Wade also came from a blue-blooded family. Forester glanced at his partner. "You think she's right? So what does it mean? The creep didn't follow her, so what?"

"It means he must have been watching her from somewhere safe," Artemis said quickly.

"Like the trees?"

Artemis was shaking her head, though. "He had a kayak with him, Cameron. He brought that white dress too. According to the coroner, h e *took* her somewhere for a couple of hours before drowning her."

Now, Forester didn't look nearly so doubtful. He stared at her, eyes wide. Wade was nodding as she spoke.

Artemis nodded once. Her fingers stopped drumming against her legs.

"What if he owns a house on the lake? Somewhere along her jogging route? What if that's how he saw her? It would give him a place to stow a kayak, to keep a kidnap victim. Give him a private way to watch her without being seen. Give him the ability to keep an eye on us and launch that kayak when he spotted us on the docks. Do we really think he just lingered around? No... No, I think he *must* own a house on the lake."

Forester was still hesitant, but seemed to be warming. He began to open his mouth to reply, but she cut him off.

"No, Cameron," she said. "It's *not* conjecture."

He closed his mouth, frowning.

"It's parallel probabilities," she said. "One way to find someone is to wait and watch, studying their moves. Another way to defeat an opponent, though," she said firmly, remembering one of her favorite games from earlier in the Seattle Open, "is to see what they've already done, retrace their steps and make an educated guess."

"So… you want us to look up lake-home owners?" Forester said.

"Specifically homes with a view of Robin's jogging route," Artemis replied quickly. She hesitated, biting her lip. "Which… I guess means someone's going to have to speak with her father…"

Forester's finger darted to his nose; he glanced at Wade. "Guess it's you, Ox. Unless you wanna send Checkers."

Wade slapped Forester's hand away and muttered, "Ms. Blythe isn't setting foot within a mile of that family." The way he said it, though, didn't seem *restrictive* so much as *protective*.

Artemis felt a jolt of gratitude at the way he nodded, sighed, and adjusted his neat, buttoned shirt. "Fine," Wade said. "I guess I'll go speak with—"

Suddenly there came a *smashing* sound through the wall—like glass shattering. A pause, then loud voices, hurried footsteps from the room next door.

Forester and Wade had reacted instantly, dropping into crouches away from the window, hands on their weapons. Wade pointed at Artemis, "Get down," he directed.

Forester, instead of trying to warn their consultant, was busy pocketing a couple of sugar packs from next to the coffee maker while simultaneously moving towards the door.

Artemis slowly lowered onto the couch again, twisting though, to look over the top and peer towards the hall.

The two agents were frowning, stepping into the hall. As the door opened, Artemis heard loud voices shouting. "He threw a brick!" someone was saying. "Go! Go!"

A few figures in brown, deputy uniforms rushed past, footsteps pounding the floor. Artemis watched, tense as Forester and Wade fell into step, slower than the others, cautious, but moving in the same direction.

For her part, she just wrinkled her nose.

Someone had thrown a brick at a police station? What sort of idiot would—

Tap. Tap. Tap.

She turned sharply, eyes wide to see a face peering through the second floor window.

14

SHE GAPED AT THE figure in the window, and he kept waving hurriedly,

His fingerless gloves tapped the frame. She recognized those mismatched eyes staring through the glass. One the color of wheat fields the other the hue of sapphire. A single, teardrop tattoo dripped from the corner of his left eye. His long hair was tied back in a ponytail, and two words tattooed along his neck, under his chin and reaching to his ears. They were in a language Artemis didn't understand, and the ink was fading from age.

Her brother, Tommy, had connections to the Seattle mob, and currently, his eyes were wide as he motioned to her with some urgency to open the window. Every few seconds, he shot a look over his shoulder, towards the ground, as if scared someone might round the building.

The sound of shattering from earlier had come from the adjoining room which faced the street, away from the parking lot where her brother now dangled.

For a brief moment, she considered simply ignoring the issue. He'd texted her a thumb's up.

She hadn't realized this was code for kicking over a hornet's nest and breaking into a police station. She could hear more voices in the hallway. The sounds of anger had now reached the front entrance.

Tommy was glaring at her now, pointing a finger at her threateningly. She sighed, pushing slowly off the couch to approach. Her brother was now pressing his head against the glass as if preparing to smash it with his skull.

She picked up the pace, hurrying forward. She slid the window open.

"Are you insane?" she said.

"Nice to see ya too, sis," Tommy muttered as he was already clambering through the window. One of his long, skinny legs straddled over the windowsill. He was wearing biker leathers with a golden skull stitched over one lapel pocket. He smelled vaguely of gasoline, and his spindly fingers—jutting past the edges of his fingerless gloves—were tapping away even as he navigated his precarious position.

Deciding she was already an accomplice in whatever Tommy had done, Artemis snagged her twin brother and yanked him further into the room, glaring all the while. She took a moment to peer into the parking lot. It didn't seem as if anyone had yet rounded the building. But she spotted movement past the small, black fence cordoning off the front entrance, and so she quickly closed the window and retreated.

She shot a hurried look towards the door to the break room, feeling a slow flush of panic.

"Tommy," she hissed, "What are you doing?"

He was dusting himself off, glancing around and admiring the place. He nodded. "Nice digs."

"Tommy," she said, realizing she was still gripping his wrist tightly, "what's the matter with you? Did you throw a brick through a police station window?"

He shrugged. "Was a rock."

"Tommy!"

He smoothed some of his wild, fly-away hair back behind an ear, studying her from his tattooed face. She wished it wasn't so, but half the time Tommy showed up, she just wanted to slap him.

Now, he was turning towards the coffee maker, but she held onto his wrist, pulling sharply. "Tommy—you can't stay! The FBI was *just* in this room."

He looked back at her, shrugged. "Just tell 'em I'm visiting."

"You came through the window!"

"Yeah, well—trouble with this station before. Desk sergeant woulda recognized me."

She let out a faint sigh, trying to calm her racing blood pressure. "What do you want?"

He stopped now, glancing at her, his eyes no longer roaming the police station's break room. At the question, he fidgeted uncomfortably, and then he yanked his arm away. "It true?"

"Is *what* true?"

"You visit dad?"

She went quiet now.

His nostrils flared. "Shit. You did. What the hell for?"

"Tommy, it's not important—look, couldn't you have called about that?"

He shook his head. "Been only using the phone for thirty seconds at a time ever since you led a horde of LEOs to my crib."

"I... I don't really know what that means. Yes, I visited dad. It was as awful as you might imagine. Is that all?"

Artemis stared at her brother, willing him to climb right back out that window.

He was scratching at his chin and shaking his head. But after a couple of hesitant glances towards her, he said, "Quick question. Why don't you tell me why you're here?"

"Did you catch that case by the orchard?"

She tensed. Any time one of her family members came within sniffing distance of a murder, she could feel her stomach tighten. "Does that matter?"

"I thought you were getting out of town."

"I thought so, too. Something came up."

"Apparently. Artemis, look, I shouldn't be here."

"At least we agree on one thing."

"But, you saved me from being arrested for a murder I didn't commit," he said, trailing off, then he frowned and quickly added, "after leading the feds right to my door."

"Tommy, whatever you've come to say, please, I'm begging you, just spit it out."

"Drop this case. I don't know what they have on you. I don't know why you keep working with these guys." He pointed a finger towards the closed door to the break room. He was scowling now. The way he said *these guys* hinted that he had wanted to use stronger language but censored himself for her sake. "But you can't investigate this one, okay."

Now, Artemis frowned. "Excuse me?"

"It's for your own good. Trust me. You don't want to mess with this one."

"I think I do." She wasn't sure why she said it. But something about her brother's attitude was rubbing her the wrong way. Not just because he had broken into a police station and used her to do it. But because something was quite clearly off.

"Tommy," she said slowly, "do you *know* something about the case?"

A flash of guilt in his eyes. But he recovered quickly rubbing at his neck tattoo with one hand. "I *know* you should stay away."

She stepped closer now, her voice firm. She grabbed her brother by the jacket. She looked him in the eyes and said, "If you know something, you better tell me. Right now."

She didn't quite stamp a foot, but the staccato of her words had a similar effect.

Her brother, though, just shook his head. He gave an innocent, little shrug. "Nothing. Look, I came here as a favor. I'm telling you, stay away."

Artemis scowled; her brother wasn't the sort to give in to bribery or begging—he wasn't the type to bend either. Under pressure, Tommy stood rigid, stubborn, or he broke. There was no give.

But he knew something; that much was obvious. The faint scent of cold enchilada lingered in the break room, mixing with coffee, and causing her stomach to turn. The sounds from further in the police station had gone silent now.

She watched her brother, reached a decision, took a step back and then shouted top of her lungs, "Help! Intruder!"

Tommy cursed, darted forward and clapped a hand across her mouth.

She tried to shove his hand away. "Intruder," she said, a bit quieter this time. Now, she was more interested in making the point than riling Tommy. Her brother glanced at the door, but Forester and Wade were still absent.

His hand smelled even more of gasoline. She had learned, though, as a child, it was best not to ask.

"Shut up," Tommy hissed, pushing her backwards, his hand against her mouth "I came here as a favor."

She knocked his hand away and then kicked him, hard in the shin. He lost his grip on her and hobbled, cursing.

He glared at her, half bent, massaging his leg. "I'm telling you," he seethed, glaring, some of his hair having fallen past his eyes. He huffed, blowing the hair, and sending it fluttering before it descended once more. "This guy—this guy who killed that girl: he's dangerous. Like obviously. But I mean really dangerous."

She stared, her skin prickling. A sudden warm flush came across her cheeks. "Do you know who it is?"

He was still massaging his shin and shooting worried glances towards the break room door. Artemis thought she heard the sound of approaching voices now, footsteps.

Tommy must have detected the noises too, because he said, in a hurried voice, "Look, it isn't much. I can't be telling you this. But if you want to get killed, stay on this case. You're not a cop, Art. You're not. You play games for a living."

She scowled at him. "And what do *you* do?"

He shook his head. "I wasn't insulting you. From me that's a compliment. Good for you. You got out of the rat race. If only we could all be so lucky. But look, my point is, something happened. A few nights ago. And it had some lieutenants spooked."

"Lieutenants?"

He nodded once.

Her eyes widened. "Mobsters?"

"High ranking guys. Tough guys. But one of their daughters was killed."

Artemis felt the blood leave her face; she had moved back so far that she now bumped into the glass. The cold, glazed surface chilled the skin on her arm. "A mobster's daughter was killed?"

"That's right. I'm not going to say who. And I'm not giving any addresses or details. Just understand, this guy was found—" He hesitated, biting his lip very much in the way Artemis so often did.

"What do you mean?"

Her brother shook his head, looking off and muttering darkly, cursing beneath his breath. "You really are something, sis."

"Just tell me, Tommy"

He looked caught. The sound of voices had now reached the break room door again. He cursed and muttered, "Tell them I'm with you."

"Tell me what I want to know. And I'll tell them whatever you want."

He glared, but then, through clenched teeth, leaning back, and trying to look casual now, he said, "This lieutenant's daughter was drowned in a pond behind the guy's house. They found her body, left there. But there were a few soldiers in the garden, so they went after the guy."

"They saw him?"

"Evidently. According to security footage from this big house, it just caught three gunmen shouting and running towards the pond. The footage didn't span the whole area."

"Tommy, who? Tell me who it is. I need to speak with these guys."

"No. You can't."

The break room door was now opening.

"Tommy, please," she insisted.

But he shook his head and said, quietly, "You can't, because the killer massacred them. Three against one. He ripped them to shreds. And I mean literally. One of the guys had all the bones in his legs crushed. They don't even know how."

Artemis stared at her brother. "How's that possible?"

Now the form of Agent Forester was sidling back through the door, talking to Wade over his shoulder.

Tommy shifted uncomfortably and said, in nearly a whisper, his eyes no longer on his sister, "He killed the daughter and then smashed three gun thugs. Get me? If he can do that, you're not safe with these two bozos. Get out."

He straightened now, leaning back against the wall next to his sister and forcing a smile, pretending to chuckle as if they had been sharing jokes.

Forester and Wade looked up at the same time. They both went still.

Tommy determinedly looked at his sister, as if there was nothing interesting about the FBI agents in the room.

Artemis wanted to hide. She was finding it difficult to track all the different sources of information. On one side, her brother had smashed a window just to warn her. He was too paranoid to call. This wasn't a problem she could solve right now.

Also, though, the two FBI agents weren't stupid. They would likely guess how Tommy had ended up in the room. But finally, her brother's warning itself caused the hairs to rise on the back of her neck. A mobster's daughter was also killed? What was going on?

The killer apparently killed three men, escaping afterward. She felt that same shiver along her neck now spread to her arms.

"Hey there," Forester said conversationally. His tone was good-humored as ever, but his eyes were fixed on Tommy.

"Mr. Blythe," Agent Wade said carefully, stepping further into the room and shooting a look into a corner of the space that hadn't been immediately visible from the door. When he found it empty, he relaxed a bit, but his eyes returned to Artemis' brother.

She shifted uncomfortably but received an elbow to the ribs from Tommy.

Prompted, she cleared her throat and said quickly, "My brother just stopped by to give me something."

Forester glanced over his shoulder, back at her. "We didn't see him pass us in the hall."

"I did," Tommy insisted. "You guys were busy with whatever you were doing."

Forester hesitated. "I see. What did you give her?"

Tommy glared, his tear-tattoo shifting. "A hug," he said.

"Right…"

Wade was looking directly at the window, frowning now.

Artemis, deciding that currently silence was giving them too much time to think, said, "Actually, Tommy has a clue on the case."

"No, I don't," he cut in.

"Mighty generous of you," Forester said, nodding. "Let's hear it."

Tommy scowled, though. "I'm not telling shit to you. Last week you put me in cuffs."

Forester nodded. "You sound just like my ex-wife."

Artemis wrinkled her nose. She hadn't known Forester had been married.

"Well, I should be going," Tommy said with a quick shrug.

Artemis wasn't sure what to do. Part of her wanted to hold him back. But another part knew that the best way to turn Tommy against her was to try and *force* him to do anything. As it was, she was lucky he'd told her what he had.

Still, at the moment, it was just a story. Nothing verified.

She watched as her brother hurried away. He slipped between the two FBI agents, nodding at both in turn. Wade tensed, and it almost looked like he was about to reach out and stop Tommy.

But Forester gave a nearly imperceptible shake of his head. Forester said, as Tommy brushed past, "Nice seeing you again."

"Die in a ditch," Tommy replied.

Forester just nodded once, as if this were the appropriate response to his farewell. Tommy pushed roughly through the break room door and then turned right.

The exit was left.

Artemis wondered if she ought to go after her brother. But there were too many things to keep track of. Maybe he was going to find another window to crawl out of to avoid the desk sergeant. Or maybe he was going to get himself arrested. She was beginning to realize she simply couldn't keep track of everything Tommy did.

"So," Forester said, glancing at her, "*that* was fun. Do you know what the word defenestration means?"

Artemis winced. "Technically, he came *through* the window."

Wade frowned. "Wait," he said. "What does defenestration mean?"

Artemis interrupted before Forester could give a vocabulary lesson to his partner. She spoke quickly, her words rushed. "Tommy said something interesting. He said a mobster's daughter was killed a few days ago. *Drowned*."

Forester tensed. Wade looked over sharply. Forester said. "He thinks it's the same guy?"

Artemis nodded. "Apparently, our case was on the local news. He thinks this guy is dangerous. He said three soldiers went after him but were killed."

Forester whistled, nodding. "Did he say who it was?"

Artemis shook her head. "I was hoping maybe something came up in a police report."

"Nothing major. We would've seen. Did your brother say where this happened?"

Artemis winced. She glanced back through the door where her brother had stomped through. "He wasn't really in the questioning mood."

Forester nodded. "He didn't seem happy to see me."

Wade said, "You *did* cuff him."

"I'm sure he doesn't really want you to die in a ditch," Artemis added, wincing on behalf of her brother's manners.

Forester waved a hand. "Don't worry about it. I mean it. He sounded exactly like my ex. So what are we doing now?"

Wade hesitated, glancing between the two of them. Artemis said, "I still think we should check owners of lake houses."

Forester pointed at Wade. "You can look through last week's ticker. A mob-guy would not have reported a murder. Especially if some of his soldiers were killed doing or possessing anything less than legal. But maybe some neighbor heard something. Check for fireworks reports. Someone could have mistaken gunshots."

"Worth checking out," Wade said. "I'll send the IR to municipalities nearby."

Forester nodded, adjusting one of his buttons and trying to line it up with the others. The tall, wild-haired man said, "Are we looking for a criminal record? Some connection with that prison?"

Artemis cut in, "I was thinking, maybe I made a mistake." As she spoke, she could feel some of her apprehension, her fear dwindling. Tommy's warning chilled her bones, but now her mind was racing. "What if this guy is getting revenge somehow? If my brother's right, and a mobster lost his daughter too... What are the odds that a mobster and cop are the two surviving fathers?"

Forester and Wade were scowling now. As she approached the door, her words came quickly. "Maybe we should check into people who had grudges against Sergeant Dawkins. Maybe this isn't about the girls at all. What if it's got to do with the judicial system somehow?"

"Someone's targeting the daughters to get at the fathers?" Forester said.

"Maybe."

Wade added, "How does this tie in with your father? What about those postcards?"

Artemis was shaking her head. "There were no other released prisoners who were associated with my dad. He might not be involved in the way I thought he was. Somehow, though, he knew about this murder."

Forester pointed at her. "Maybe you should start considering the fact that he–"

"I promise you, he's not psychic. But," she said, slowly, frowning, "he is getting his information somewhere. Which means, these crimes were not crimes of opportunity. They were planned. Meticulous. Someone has been keeping track of these girls. I still think we should check the lake homes. As for the postcards, I'm still working on that a ngle."

Wade and Forester shared a look. Wade looked uncertain. Forester, though, just shrugged. "Suit yourself," he said with a nod. "I'm driving. Wade, you can make the calls this time."

"I always make the calls."

Forester tapped his nose and pointed and then pushed back out of the break room door. The tall agent hesitated in the hall, glancing in the direction where Tommy had disappeared. There was no further sign of her brother. But then, Forester shrugged, shook his head, and stomped off in the other direction towards the exit.

Artemis wasn't sure if she should be grateful for this or concerned. But right now, her skin was prickling. A killer had targeted a mobster's daughter and a cop's daughter. Her father said he was going to kill more. But if Tommy was right, then he had *already* killed. Which meant her father was wrong about the timing of the murders. There were not *nine* to go. But eight.

What if her father wasn't behind it at all?

But what about the postcards? How did Joseph Baker and his jumbled notes play into all of this?

She sighed in frustration. First things first, she decided. There were too many questions. Right now, the best way to find answers was to follow the lead.

As she moved forward, she said, slowly, "One thing we should look for in these lake houses," she said. "Mobster affiliation. I'm sure you guys track that sort of thing. I want to know if anyone on the jogging route that Robin took is in any way associated with organized crime."

Forester smirked. "You're beginning to sound like you're field-trained there, Checkers."

She muttered darkly at this comment as the three of them reached the exit to the police station and stepped out into the sunlight, picking up the pace with each hurried footfall.

15

Artemis sat in the backseat again, feeling her stomach clench. She scowled at her phone, shaking, her thumb grazing the smooth screen. Her cheek pressed against the window, the glass warmed by the sun. Now, out of the corner of her eye, over the passing trees, Artemis watched the sun slowly dip beyond the mountains.

Forester's window was open, allowing the faint breeze to trickle into the backseat. They were leaving the main road and turning onto another lakeside driveway.

She had listened as Agent Wade placed necessary calls while entering information on his laptop which he had connected to his hotspot.

And though, occasionally, she glanced over his shoulder to watch what he was typing, Artemis focused on little else than her own puzzle.

The postcards from Baker to her father.

But there was no pattern. She'd read and reread each postcard multiple times. Now, she had visual snapshots in her mind of each card.

But none of it made sense. She knew she was missing something. She had tried corresponding the pictures to the text. Tried different word replacement keys. Tried switching sentences for numbers. She had tried everything she could think of, but none of it worked.

She gritted her teeth, her thumb grazing the glass faster, *faster*. One hand twisted against the seat belt over her chest.

"That's really bugging you, isn't it?" Forester said, glancing into the rearview mirror.

Artemis shot a look into the reflective glass then glanced back at her phone. "I'll figure it out," she insisted. She didn't feel nearly as confident as she sounded.

"Rare, isn't it? To find something you can't outsmart," said Forester.

She looked up again, wrinkling her nose. This was not a subject she wanted to broach, so instead she went on the attack. "You drive too slow."

Forester didn't exactly follow the stream of traffic. This man was the definition of marching to a beat of his own drum. And that beat was of a lower tempo than most. The vehicle trundled along, and through the open window at Forester's side, faint gusts of wind carried the scent of lake water and vegetation through the window.

Inhaling the fragrance, Artemis shifted in her back seat and found she was able to relax, at least a little.

"What about you, Wade?" Forester said. "Which one is it?"

Artemis looked up now as well. In the drive over, Wade had managed to whittle down two of the houses on Robin's jogging path to potential mob connections.

Now he was shaking his head. "Hard to tell. The Organized Crime detail has some things on Mr. Smith. Besides, look at the name. *Smith*."

"First name?" Forester asked.

Wade wrinkled his nose, the keyboard clacking on his lap, and then he said, "Greg. His name is Greg Smith. He has more than two offshore banking accounts, and he's failed to file taxes for nearly three years. On top of that, about a year ago, he was indicted on a weapons charge. But he never showed up."

"He still owns the house?"

"It's currently being haggled over—government wants it. Bank wants it too. It's a mess."

Forester said, "But it was near enough to Robin's jogging route?"

Wade nodded.

"So who's the second option? Also an alias?"

"I don't think so. We have a long paper trail for Mr. Jones; he's ex-military by the looks of things and came back to Seattle about ten years ago. He was employed for three of those years, but then, out of nowhere, he quit."

"Any government assistance?"

"No unemployment, nothing," said Wade, still frowning.

Forester was shaking his head in the front seat. "Do we have a criminal record on the guy?"

Wade nodded. "Arrested a few times for assault. Racketeering is the assumption, but nothing's been proven. They tried to build a case against him and his uncle, but nothing stuck."

"His uncle?" Artemis asked.

Wade nodded once. "He lives with his uncle. The house is owned by the older Mika Jones. Mika is definitely mob; he served about eight years for homicide, but it was ruled involuntary manslaughter; he got off light."

"So maybe we visit the Jones family first," Forester said. "And if nothing comes up, we can check out Smith's uninhabited residence."

Wade replied, "That's what I was thinking. I'm already sending a unit over to the Smith home, just in case."

Forester picked up the speed a little, along the road circling the lake, agitating a cloud of dust.

Artemis could feel her anxiety mounting as they moved around the large body of water. Pinelake was situated on the southern tip of the sharpest portion of the lake. But there were other towns, and homes, settled along the shore of the ten-thousand-acre lake.

She was thinking of what her brother had said, if he could be believed. The killer had targeted a mobster's daughter.

"Did we hear anything back about gunshots or fireworks, or a reported body a few days ago?" Artemis enquired.

Forester glanced in the mirror. "Agent Grant is checking that out. I haven't heard from her, so I'm guessing there's nothing yet."

Wade nodded with this assumption. Artemis leaned back. "So that means no one reported anything explicitly."

Forester shook his head. "It's mob. I wouldn't expect anything different. Grant will find it. If there's anything, even a hint of some gunfight, she'll figure it out."

Artemis returned her attention to her phone, still frowning.

They moved around the lake, and Agent Wade entered the information for the address on the GPS.

Artemis knew they needed something more concrete than means and opportunity.

Forester glanced in the backseat. "This time we're going to park a block away, and I'm locking the doors. Sound good?"

Artemis nodded.

"All you have to do is stay put. Don't open the doors. Can you do that?"

"I think I might be able to figure it out."

Forester flashed a thumbs up in the mirror. Wade looked uncomfortable, shaking his head.

Artemis exhaled faintly. The small, purple line on the GPS was getting smaller, and smaller...

***

Artemis peered through the windshield, sitting on the side of the road and watching as the two FBI agents entered the large silver gate.

She shifted uncomfortably, twisting at the restrictive seatbelt tight to her chest.

This time, she had made sure Forester didn't leave the keys in the ignition. The doors to the vehicle were locked.

She bit her lip nervously, glancing towards the rearview mirror and glimpsing the faint swish and sway of blue waters beneath the last vestiges of sunlight.

The horizon streaked pink and orange, competing with the forest canopy for a resplendent panorama.

She watched as two men in black suits flanked the FBI agents at the top of the hill, leading them from the guardhouse further in to the large estate.

The giant mansion beyond the silver gate was difficult to make out. Not because she couldn't see it. But because she couldn't see *most* of it. The thing sprawled across the lake shore, ducking in and out of trees.

The gray stone and blue shingle, with more than one turret, made the thing look like something out of a fairy tale. A dock led across the

162

waters, visible just around the side of a red brick wall. The silver gate itself was topped with small pieces of quartz and glass, which reflected the light like shimmering gemstones on a crown. The whole spectacle was quite impressive.

As her eyes darted one way then the other, trying to take it all in, she was grateful she was allowed to stay back in the car.

At least, grateful for the first few seconds.

Then she started wondering if perhaps she was going to wait a while.

She frowned now, staring through the silver bars and peering up at the large house.

Forester had offered to leave a weapon with her. Agent Wade had expressly forbidden it.

Artemis suspected he'd been given instructions on this front.

Forester still would have likely slipped her a gun, but she had flat out refused. Weapons were not her realm.

The same could not be said for the men in black suits who were now returning to the guardhouse.

Occasionally, the thick set men glanced in her direction. One of them scowled.

She looked quickly away.

She shifted uncomfortably at the bottom of the asphalt driveway.

Forester and Wade were supposed to interview the Jones men about the murder.

But Artemis was now thinking about her brother; had he really come just to warn her about this strange killer? A man apparently targeting the daughters of powerful people.

Who would he attack next?

It wasn't quite like Tommy to do something purely altruistically, either. Why had he turned down the right side of the hall?

At the time, it had seemed the least important part of that interaction.

But now that she ran over it, she was analyzing it like she might a match, looking for tactical errors.

She sighed. The problem with thinking strategically where Tommy was concerned was that he did not.

Tommy made choices based on how he was feeling at the time. He was a scrapper, stubborn to a fault, and, as she was continuing to realize, an absolute pain in the ass.

She shook her head, looking down at her phone again.

She had given up on the postcards for now. Something was missing. There was some piece she hadn't figured out yet. Did her father have some sort of physical key?

This was the only solution she could think of.

Artemis tried to push this from her mind. She had time for a chess match online if she wanted.

She considered calling her friends, the Washingtons…

Then she saw movement. Artemis hesitated, shifting, and glancing in the mirror.

She saw it again. *Movement* on the water.

She turned now, fully, peering through the rear window.

What was that?

It seemed to be coming closer, slowly.

Was that a jet ski?

She wrinkled her nose and shot a look up the hill. The mobsters in the guardhouse were paying attention as well.

They were far enough away, though, that she risked pushing out the back door. The locks clicked as she pulled the handle, and she stepped onto the tarmac at the bottom of the long driveway. She turned her back to the fairytale lake home.

Her eyes were fixed on the jet ski instead.

It continued to spin in lazy circles while slowly approaching.

She stared, still frowning.

There was no driver. No one within line of sight, either. As evening fell, lake activities were slowly isolated to private docks or favorite shorelines.

All except the jet ski.

She stepped off the asphalt onto the leafy ground.

This gave her a better look, avoiding a particularly large tree, whose tangled roots stretched into the water.

Leaves crunched beneath her feet. The scent of earth hovered on the air. She waved a hand in front of her face to chase away mosquitoes buzzing past her skin.

All the while, she stared at the jet ski.

With a faint humming of the engine, it continued to circle itself while also inching closer to the shore. She picked up her pace now, hurrying forward, across the street, down to the water.

The ground was softer here, the mud indenting beneath her steps. She tried to avoid the root humps, nudged a fallen branch aside, and glanced up for widowmakers.

Growing up in this place, she had spent most of her time indoors. But her brother would occasionally share things he had learned in the two months he had spent with the Boy Scouts.

He had only made it two months, as he had decided the scout camping trip was the perfect opportunity to try and rob one of the instructors' homes.

But one thing he had mentioned was that a widowmaker was a branch in the high boughs of a tree. A dead branch, a large branch, that would fall if persuaded by wind or motion. According to her brother, it was the branches you didn't see that were the most dangerous. But all you had to do was look up. A shift in perspective.

And so, remembering this piece of advice, she cautiously moved down to the very edge of the water and stared at the rotating jet ski.

Fifteen feet from the shore, still moving so very slowly. Ten feet. Five. Four.

It moved in lazy, looping circles, sending water swishing out in waves. The disturbed liquid lapped against the tree roots in the muddy embankment.

"Artemis?" Forester's voice called out from behind her.

"Ms. Blythe?" Wade shouted.

"I'm fine," she shouted back. "Over here." She raised a hand and waved it at the sky.

She heard muttering, footsteps. At least this suggested things hadn't ended in a shootout in the mobster's mansion.

And then she spotted the source of the strange motion from the jet ski.

A rope. Tied to one of the handles and tilting the machine to one side.

Someone had taped the throttle, allowing it to go slowly enough so it would spin, but fast enough so it would still have forward momentum.

Suddenly, she felt a faint shiver.

Artemis spotted something else.

At the end of the rope, a white, fluttering something.

She peered into the water, frowning; near the shore where algae or scattered leaves would gather, obscuring her vision, and concealing the depths.

But suddenly the jet ski bumped against the shoreline.

More tremors in the water.

Those same tremors seemed to have now spread to Artemis' fingers.

She stared, eyes wide.

"Guys!" she called out, her voice shaking.

She could hear the sound of their feet hitting leaves, suggesting they had crossed the road as well. But she didn't look back. She was staring beneath the water, staring at the white gown fluttering under the surface of the lake.

And most of all, staring beneath the jet ski at the trapped figure of the dead woman with a rope wrapped around her neck.

16

SIRENS WAILED IN THE distance, and Artemis stood amidst the trees, trying to keep out of the way. She swallowed, her throat dry. Her eyes lingered on the white tarp and the forensic unit moving in waders near the now docile jet ski.

Red and blue lights flashed about the road, illuminating figures as evening introduced itself to the horizon. The sun, as if hiding its eyes from the horrible scene, had finally dipped beyond the mountains. Darkness approached quickly, and Artemis' skin prickled with chill wind, goosebumps rising along her arms and cheeks.

She shifted uncomfortably beneath the branches, one shoulder scraping against the rough wood of the bark. Small, brown fragments tumbled onto her shoulder, and she flicked the curls of wood off with her fingers.

Her eyes never left the body.

Forester was moving along the shore, speaking to Agent Grant.

The snow-haired woman had a way of appearing and disappearing like a mirage. Now, as she moved next to Forester, her face was gaunt, her lips pressed tightly together, as if something were ready to rupture.

Agent Wade was busy helping some of the other cops to bring the jet ski to shore. Artemis lingered off to the side, wondering if it was best for her to make herself scarce. Sergeant Dawkins hadn't shown up. But other members from the family had: namely, Ross Dawkins, the bald man with no neck, and his brother, Merl Dawkins, who was almost comically opposite to his large-framed kin, with reedy features and a thin face. Merl and Ross were occasionally shooting glances in Artemis' direction.

It hadn't helped that when they'd first arrived, the initial responders had gestured to Artemis and told the Dawkins brothers, "She found the body."

Ross' face had prickled with strange hues of crimson, his eyes flashing murderously. "Of course she found it," he'd muttered to Merl. His thin, mullet-sporting brother had sighed, adjusting his black-rimmed glasses but adding nothing to the implicit accusation.

Artemis was struggling to focus, her eyes on the corpse, but her mind spinning.

What were they missing?

The killer was keeping track of them—that much seemed obvious. How else would he have known when to propel that kayak, or the jet ski? The police had already run the jet ski. Reported stolen two days ago.

Artemis tucked her hands inside her sleeves, massaging her forearms, and biting her lower lip. The young woman couldn't have been much older than twenty. As of yet, they had no identification. She was barefoot, like Robin Dawkins had been, and she wore the same gossamer-thin, drenched white gown.

What was the significance of the white?

Artemis frowned.

Only one obvious answer came to mind. A wedding?

Was the killer somehow... marrying them before drowning them? She shook her head in disgust. Psychology was *not* her specialty. Human behavior, human instinct *was*. But the truly twisted, strange machinations of mammalian minds were beyond her realm of expertise.

Still... she'd come this far. She needed to bring *something* of use to Agent Grant.

At this point, Artemis wouldn't have been surprised if Grant, like the rest of the police force, started wondering if Artemis was somehow involved.

She pushed away from the tree now, fingers rubbing against the rough bark. She peered at the body on the ground, specifically staring at the noose wrapped around the woman's neck. It had been used to secure and tilt the jet ski's handles. She'd been attached to the bottom of the watercraft with wire, the same way Robin had been.

A grotesque spectacle.

What did it all mean?

What was the killer getting at?

Not Joseph Baker—he was in custody and her father was behind bars.

What if her newer suspicions were correct, and what if her father had nothing to do with these murders?

So how had he known about them?

She shifted uncomfortably, huffing air, and shaking her head. Something about the rope struck her as somewhat odd. She stared at the knot used to wrap around the jet ski's rubber handle.

It was an *odd* knot. Multiple loops and a strange sort of bulge at the end. She'd never seen its kind before. She took mental snapshot of the knot, determined to file the information under "further use."

And then, she turned sharply on her heel and began marching back up the hill in the direction of the giant, mobster mansion.

If they wanted more information, she needed to find out if Tommy had been telling the truth about a mobster's daughter. The coroner, Dr. Bryant, was still on her way to the scene. They were still attempting to identify the victim. Police were combing the lakeshore, but Artemis knew—like last time—they'd be late.

No... No, if she wanted to unearth something on this case, she was going to have to do some dirty digging.

No more cowering in cars, behind locked doors.

Another woman was dead.

Another killer targeting the helpless.

Artemis' teeth pressed together. Part of her mind wanted to flit away to *another* young woman. A thirteen-year-old girl... Helen Blythe had gone missing in the mountains visible across the lake.

And for the first time...

Artemis was wondering if her father was telling the truth.

Perhaps he didn't have anything to do with Helen's disappearance?

He was the Ghostkiller—a serial killer. The evidence was overwhelming. But perhaps he was right about Helen.

What if she was still alive?

What if her disappearance had *triggered* his murder spree? He'd killed young women who were smart, beautiful, academically inclined—just like Helen.

Artemis shook her head, scarcely daring to let her hopes rise. She couldn't afford to allow her emotions to get the best of her.

No... No, not now. For all she knew, her father was playing her. Just because he repeated a lie over and over didn't mean it was any more likely to be true.

In the same way, until she knew beyond a shadow of a doubt her father *wasn't* involved with this case... then she refused to second-guess her initial assumptions.

He had known about the body at the docks. Had *known* about this new killer.

Just because she couldn't figure out *how* he was connected, didn't mean the Ghostkiller was absolved of anything. Beyond that, she would find out the key to those postcards. One way or another, she was determined. In fact, later that night, she'd scheduled a meeting with the Washingtons. If anyone could help her crack the cipher, it was her analysts. Each of them a chess master in their own right.

But now...

She picked up the pace, leaving the detritus, the leaf scattered ground, and moving hastily onto the tarmac of the long, black driveway curling to the silver gates.

Police on either side of the road watched her go. She pointed and called to the one scowling at her the least. "I'm going up there. If I don't come back, tell Agent Grant."

And then she turned sharply, dark hair swishing across her pale face. Her mismatched eyes glared at the two men in black suits lingering in the guardhouse. They hadn't left their position in more than an hour. The arrival of a host of cops outside their boss's home had only put them on edge.

Earlier, Artemis had seen another dark car roll up the driveway and enter through the silver gates. Backup, she'd guessed at the time.

She wondered if they'd be more or less jumpy if they knew the cops weren't there for them.

But the thing she knew about a properly executed bluff: the more assumptions people made, the better.

And right now, they were starving for information, and she was sick of feeling useless.

As she neared the gate, the two men in the guardhouse perked up. She heard a faint *creak* of old hinges as the door opened. A white, plastic frame around what looked like thick, bulletproof glass. The man shifted as he stepped out of the guardhouse, frowning at her, his eyes bright in the evening.

"You a cop?" he called.

She shook her head. "Consultant."

His frown didn't change. "What's going on down there?" he asked.

"I need to speak with both of you," she said, she gestured towards the other guard, waving her hand authoritatively.

Of course, she *had* no authority. She didn't even have a badge. If anything, she was being forced to help by the FBI. At this point, though, she felt fairly certain that if she'd attempted to leave, no one would stop her.

But she was invested in seeing this through. Other young women had died fifteen years ago. She hadn't been able to do a thing then. She still didn't know if her father was involved, but one way or another, she was going to stop the bastard responsible.

The second guard hesitated, glancing at her raised hand and looking towards his partner. The first guard was neatly dressed in a dark suit with silver sideburns and eyes like a snake's. There was *nothing* warm about his countenance. He had a holster displayed on his belt, but the weapon was conspicuously missing. She wondered if the visitors at the end of the drive had anything to do with that.

The man with the dead eyes finally nodded to his partner, jerking his head towards Artemis.

The second figure emerged from the guardhouse. He had to turn sideways to do it. The door frame simply wasn't wide enough for his shoulders. She stared, stunned, as steroids with a personality and a comb over emerged from the small cubicle.

The man had more muscles than Artemis had regrets. His shoulders were larger than her head. The man eyed her now, his thick chest threatening to pop the top button of his sleek, black suit. He looked a bit like a football player... if that football player had eaten another linebacker.

When he spoke, he had a strange, soothing voice. Like a jazz singer, or a masseuse trying not to disturb the mood.

"So what's going on down there?" he said in that calming, smooth voice.

The second man with the dead eyes looked back. Both of them, now that she came to a stop a foot away from the metal bars, smelled faintly of expensive aftershave. Neither of them wore any jewelry, and they were both glaring at her.

Though, granted, Ross Dawkins' glare had been far more hateful.

Artemis countered with a question of her own, trying her best not to tremble. "Do either of you have connections with Seattle?" she said.

Neither of them blinked.

She let out a long huff. "Are either of you aware of a lieutenant's daughter drowning? A shoot-out afterwards?"

She studied their faces closely. But neither really reacted. They just watched her, frowning. She let out a faint puff of air. "I'm not here to cause trouble," she said quickly. "I'm not here for you or your boss, or whoever showed up an hour ago in that tinted sedan.

Now Mr. Steroids and Mr. Snake were beginning to turn away.

Steroids shook his head, murmuring in that soft voice, "I'm afraid you're at the wrong house. Please remove yourself from the driveway. This is private property." The lines sounded rehearsed.

Artemis couldn't tell if either of them had recognized anything in her words. She huffed in frustration and leaned forward, slapping her hands against the silver bars. As she did, she noticed a blinking red light flash above her—a camera, watching. She wrinkled her nose, but, fingers still pressed to the cold bars, she said insistently, "Unless you want to come with me, you'll tell me what I need to know."

Snake-eyes snorted. "No gun, doll. No badge. You ain't a cop. You ain't a fed. Don't really know what a consultant is, neither. Get lost."

She bit her lip, mumbling beneath her breath to try and calm her rising anxiety. "E4. E5. Knight F3. H6..."

"What was that?" the steroid-using guard snapped.

Artemis, though, took this as an invitation to try again. "Please," she insisted. "You *need* to tell me. Whoever killed that lieutenant's daughter—"

"Lady!" snapped the man. "No one's daughter died here. I don't know about this lieutenant business. But if you're talking Seattle, you'd best talk to Seattle. Get me? We're not affiliated with those scumbags."

Artemis blinked, leaning back, hands still pressed to the gate. "You're not?" She frowned. She supposed this made sense. She didn't know all the inner-workings of the underground, criminal world her brother was a part of. Tommy hadn't said *which* family or outfit was attacked three nights ago.

Hell... She didn't even know who *Tommy* worked for.

She could feel her heart racing, but she tried to keep it in check, stuttering at first, then shooting a glance down the hill. A few of the police cars were moving away now, making room for an ambulance. She'd lost sight of Forester and Grant, but she wondered if now was the time to try and incite a bit more leverage. Clearly, neither of these men would tell her anything.

If they even know anything, a voice whispered in her mind. Maybe they didn't have a clue about this alleged attack.

Or maybe... she shivered... Maybe Tommy had made the whole damn thing up.

Artemis shivered, standing in the dark, outside a mobster's mansion. She didn't know what else to say. With a frustrated sigh, she began to turn.

But as she did, the black speaker set in the wall suddenly crackled. The red light from the camera continued to blink. It may have been her imagination, but it almost felt as if the camera moved, emitting a faint whirring sound.

"What is your name, lady?" said a voice over the speaker.

It was difficult to make out much about the voice due to the static, the hum of voices behind her, and her own terror surging through her chest.

Artemis summoned what little resolve she had left. She swallowed, feeling her mouth suddenly dry. "Artemis," she said quietly.

"You have a last name, Artemis?" said the voice over the speaker.

Artemis hesitated but then deciding that, in this place, volunteering her family name wasn't the best course of action, she said, "Do you know anything about an attack three days ago?"

Suddenly, the gate buzzed. The two guards looked surprised, glancing sharply at each other as if wondering who had pressed the button.

But then the voice over the speaker said, "Bring her in. I'll meet her by the pool, and avoid Jasper; I haven't fed him yet."

Artemis hesitated. The gate slowly swung inwards.

She shot a look down the driveway towards the others.

She could no longer see familiar faces. The ambulance was now leaving. A couple of the police cars followed in an escort pattern. Someone had managed to load the jet ski onto a trailer. This was also pulling away but heading in the opposite direction around the lake.

The mobsters noticed her attention. Snake-eyes said, "No cops."

Artemis felt a flash of fear. Standing there on the cold asphalt, in front of a slowly opening gate, under the dark of night, she wondered if she was making a horrible mistake. Then again, they needed more information. Her father had said the killer was going to kill ten times. If Tommy was right, that meant there were seven girls left.

Seven young women like Robin. Seven young women like Helen.

Artemis found her teeth clenching. One of her hands shook so badly, she jammed it into her pocket. "All right," she said shakily. "I can't be long, I told them where I was."

"You coming or not?" snapped the man with the silver temples.

She let out a huff but then hurriedly stepped through the opening gate, onto the smooth path that led up to the front door of the enormous house.

The moment she crossed the threshold, as if motion activated, the doors began to close again.

Artemis found a knot in her stomach threatening to spread.

The two mobsters were looking at each other, and one of them raised an eyebrow.

The one with dead eyes said, "You want to close up, or you want to take her and deal with Jasper?"

Steroids shrugged and then, without answering, slipped back into the guardhouse.

The first guard sighed, shaking his head and muttering. Then, he gestured at Artemis, "Follow me. Don't touch anything. Don't record anything. If I sniff a wire or a camera, we're going to have issues. Got it?"

"Yes," she said quickly. "What's your name?"

He shook his head. "No name. Come on. Also, don't step into anything that looks like pudding. Jasper's been having some intestinal issues."

Artemis wrinkled her nose, her eyes darting to watch the ground carefully. She wondered as she did, because of the man who had sired her, if a comment like this was simply designed to redirect her attention away from the house and the man leading her.

She decided she didn't much care.

If the person on the intercom had something useful, this was the only path forward.

She shot another look back through the silver gate and said, a bit more firmly, "I can't be long, because ..."

"They know where you are," the guard cut her off. "Heard you the first time."

Artemis watched the side of his face, her eyes straining in the dark as he picked up the pace. Even the walk from the gate to the front doors was a stretch. But he didn't lead her to the doors. Instead, avoiding a couple of patches of the aforementioned droppings, she followed the guard around one of the many sides of the enormous mansion.

She had seen hotels that were smaller.

"What type of animal is Jasper?" She said as they moved past another pile of droppings. Her skin prickled with unease. "Not an alligator or tiger or something, is it?"

The mobster snorted. "Jasper is a dog."

"A doberman? A rottweiler?"

"You'll see."

Artemis couldn't help her imagination from going wild. As she picked up the pace, hastening after her guide, she thought she detected the faint scent of chlorine. A welcome odor compared to what she'd been inhaling before.

The guard led her around another wing of the enormous home. And then he paused, pointing. "Boss is back there. I have to frisk you."

Artemis stared at him. "You're not touching me."

The guard glared. "Think you have a choice?"

She felt another flash of panic. "I'm with the FBI."

He shook his head. "No badge. You want to talk to the boss or not?"

Artemis felt another series of shivers. "I'm not armed."

"I'll just take your word for it."

"I'd appreciate that."

"Being sarcastic. Now do you want to do this the hard way or the easy way?"

Artemis couldn't quite think of an easy way of allowing a strange man to run his hands over her body. She hadn't been touched by a man like that since, well, as embarrassing as it was to admit, since Jamie Kramer. She often avoided air travel for this reason. She had taken the bus from Salinas to Seattle.

She shifted uncomfortably, realizing the guard had waited until they were in the shadows of the mansion, far enough away from the gate to propose this.

She scowled at him and wanted to protest further.

But then a voice called out from around the edge of the house. "What's taking so long?"

"I think she's carrying," the guard shouted back.

"I'm not," Artemis yelled.

"Do I need to deal with her?" the guard called out, his voice loud, casual, as if commenting on the weather. But his eyes were fixed on her, as cold as chips of ice.

Artemis was beginning to regret refusing that weapon from Forester

But then, the new voice said, "Don't be silly. That's Artemis Blythe. She's Pinelake royalty. Come on, hurry up. Jasper needs a walk in a little bit."

The guard shrugged, frowned at Artemis, but they began to move again. Artemis let out a faint sigh of relief, her hands still jammed deeply in her pocket.

She was clutching her phone. Though she wasn't sure how useful it would have been. Perhaps she would have used it as a brick to strike.

One of these days, she was going to have to figure out a way to either avoid these run-ins with dead bodies or learn something about defending herself from creeps.

Though these thoughts dissipated like fog in heat as she emerged in front of a large infinity pool. Beyond the pool was a figure sitting in a jacuzzi: a woman, wearing a modest one-piece bathing suit. A yard away a bathrobe was draped over a chair, and sitting on the bathrobe, right next to the jacuzzi, was a very small, and very fluffy dog.

The small creature got one look at Artemis and then made a yipping sound before burying its head beneath its tiny paws.

"Don't mind Jasper," the woman in the Jacuzzi said, "he's home-schooled. He's not used to strangers."

Artemis swallowed, and then the woman crooked one finger, beckoning. "Join me," she said.

Artemis hoped she just meant proximity, not the jacuzzi. Hesitantly, prompted by a nudge from the guard behind her, she approached the hot tub.

It hadn't sounded like she would be able to speak with anyone if she had tried to bring the FBI. It had been a risk. But now, Artemis was beginning to wonder...

Maybe this had been a bad idea.

17

Artemis moved slowly along the edge of the swimming pool. One side of the pool faced an incline, and the water was held back only by a glass wall. She watched where the water filtered through what looked like vents but was then recycled through small, marble fountains shaped like tulips, spread around the corners of the pool.

The fountains were illuminated by red and blue and green lights.

As Artemis moved, her eyes darted once again towards the woman in the hot tub.

She looked to be in her forties, though, it was hard to tell because of her hair. She had none. Faint droplets of water tinged the fuzz like dew drops. The woman leaned back in her jacuzzi, head resting against a small, tasseled, waterproof pillow she had placed behind her on a ledge.

Her hand occasionally stroked the small, fluffy puppy. Whenever she did, the creature would wag its tail slowly, a small pink tongue darting out to lick at the towel it rested on. But then it would spot Artemis moving and return to hiding its face, paws draped over its snout.

"I couldn't help but hear your question at the gate," the woman in the jacuzzi said.

Artemis shot a look back towards where one of the guards was now moving around the side of the house again, leaving the two of them in privacy.

"I'm afraid I don't know who you are," Artemis said, "but it sounds like you know me."

The woman nodded. "I grew up around here. I was away at college at the time, but I heard about what happened to your family—a very unfortunate circumstance." She continued to pet the small puppy. When her fingers moved, droplets of water from the jacuzzi scattered.

"You mentioned you might want to talk," Artemis said.

The woman nodded once. "First things first. How did you hear about the attack?"

"So you're aware?"

"A business partner of mine. In the city. He mentioned it..." She trailed off and smiled. She had pleasant features. They were not beautiful nor particularly symmetrical. The chin was too round. The nose slightly crooked. But her eyes were bright, intelligent. The bristle along her head was dark.

Her other hand held a small wine glass filled with red liquid and two sloshing ice cubes.

Artemis glanced beyond the swimming pool towards a black gate circling the compound. Trees rustled above the metal fence, and Artemis heard the sound of vehicles swishing by below, at the base of the incline, along the road.

"Who are you?" Artemis said.

"You can call me Sophie," the woman replied.

"Is that your name?"

She laughed. "Are you always this suspicious?"

"Only with strangers who work for the mob."

Artemis shifted uncomfortably the moment she said it. If she wasn't careful, she was going to needlessly antagonize the woman.

"Who says I work for them?"

Artemis shook her head. "Are you saying you don't?"

The woman frowned now. "I'm saying the mob works for me."

Artemis met the woman's gaze and spotted something in her eyes that Artemis didn't recognize at first. It took her a moment.... studying the woman's posture, her arms outspread, one hand stroking her pet, the other one tilting a wine glass.

And then Artemis realized what it was.

Self-confidence. But not in the way online influencers talked about.

This woman was not projecting confidence intended to impress. It was not the confidence of someone more interested in others' perception than in themselves.

It was something else. Something in the posture, the tilt of the head. This was not a beautiful woman. A crooked nose and a shaved head. She wore a one-piece swimming suit, and the form beneath was hardly flattered. She wasn't fat, but she wasn't skinny either. She didn't wear a ring on either hand, and the small, sickly puppy she kept petting looked to be the only companion she had in that giant mansion—then again, Artemis still hadn't spotted that sedan she had seen earlier.

And yet the woman seemed, in a way, content. Self-confident. The emphasis was on the *self*.

It was fascinating to Artemis as she had spent much of her life attempting to gain what this woman in the hot tub seemed to emanate.

Artemis did it through her craft. Through strategy, through winning. She was slowly becoming known in the chess community. People would now tune in to watch her stream online. Though it had been nearly a week since she'd had the chance.

But Artemis had always felt as though something was off. Something, though it was hard to pinpoint, lacking.

She wasn't sure if it was because of the way she'd been brought up. From trauma and her childhood. From the way she had been practically chased out of town.

From her father. Her missing sister. Her brother.

And yet, that woman, sitting in the tub communicated a gravitas that instantly made Artemis take a step closer. She tilted her head quizzically.

"So what do you *know*?" Sophie said. "And *who* have you been talking to?"

Artemis shook her head. "No one."

The woman grinned. "Liar."

Artemis swallowed but tried to pass it off as clearing her throat.

Then Sophie said, slowly, "*Tommy*, isn't that your brother's name? I remember him too."

Artemis frowned, feeling a shiver. "Have you been looking up my family?"

"No, dear. Fifteen years is a long time for some." She tapped a finger to her forehead. A few droplets of warm water from the hissing, bubbling, steaming jacuzzi slipped down her face. "But I don't forget."

Artemis resisted the urge to now take a step back. She avoided a patch of water that had missed one of the vents, spreading along the ground towards a small bed of roses.

The scent of chlorine lingered, and Artemis' nose itched. She adjusted her sleeves, feeling as if they were suddenly heavier now from the damp air.

"I suppose it isn't important where you heard it," said the woman. "They're partners, not family. But you should tell your brother," said the woman, conversationally, "he should keep his mouth shut if he knows what's good for him."

Artemis wasn't sure if the woman was being benevolent or simply fishing. So she kept her tone impassive. "Tommy didn't tell me anything."

The woman didn't react at first. She just watched Artemis. And then, she said, "It's important that you make sure you find out who did this."

It was Artemis' turn to remain statuesque.

Sophie continued, "The girl who was killed was only nineteen years old. She was home from college for a week. Her father, Guillermo, works for an old auto shop in Seattle. They tend to deal *mostly* in cars. Do you understand?"

Artemis nodded once.

The woman continued. "Guillermo's daughter was alone in her house. Her father was out on a business trip. He was coming back later that night. But she had been left, according to Guillermo, with three interns."

"Soldiers?"

Sophie insisted, "Interns."

Artemis frowned. "I would think it strange for a mobster to leave interns alone with his daughter."

Sophie shook her head. "Make of it what you will. Guillermo does things differently. My point isn't that they were hardly his most prolific associates."

"Where was everyone else?"

Sophie grinned. "Meeting with me, in fact. A deal that went marvelously well. Champagne all around. Except one thing. I got home and, about an hour later, received a call. The deal was off. So imagine my surprise after what I considered to be one of the best sales pitches I ever made, to find out that Guillermo is going back on his word."

Her eyes flashed. And for a moment, Artemis felt as if she found herself watching a storm cross the woman's face.

Her dark countenance shifted, and her hand went tense against her puppy. She seemed to realize she was stroking too hard though, and lifted her hand, making a small soothing noise towards her animal before looking at Artemis again. "Now, dear, listen to me. Whoever did this, according to one of my sources, also killed those three interns."

"Before or after he killed the daughter?"

"After. Unarmed, I might add."

Artemis frowned. "How do you know all this?"

The woman just shook her head. "That's not how this works. I'll answer some questions. Others have nothing to do with you. Which, I should say, we need to be clear. I'm providing you this information. But I need you to give me a guarantee that you'll be able to do something with it."

Artemis felt like she was receiving orders from a queen. She didn't like the sensation. She swallowed, and said, "Is there anything else? This Guillermo, what's his first name?"

"Raul. And one other thing."

Artemis nodded.

The woman pushed slowly out of the hot tub, reaching for her bathrobe. Distractedly, offhand, as if it were simply a throwaway phrase, she said, "If I find out that my name is used in association with this in any way, I'm going to kill your brother, and then I'm going to find you and feed him to you. Is that clear?" She looked over and smiled. That confident look in her eyes had turned somewhat rigid.

Artemis stared back. She wanted to retort. To make a threat of her own. The spike of fear in her stomach felt like shards of ice piercing her intestines. She was tired of being threatened. Tired of psychopaths.

But then, she bit back any reply. This woman knew who Artemis was, but Artemis had never heard of her before. Information was queen.

So she just said, "Let's hope it doesn't come to any of that. Thank you for your time." And she turned to walk away. She moved quickly, before she could be dismissed like some schoolchild in the principal's office.

It was the small things that most rankled.

Then again, being threatened with the death of her brother and forced cannibalism was hardly small.

Part of her wanted to call the FBI down on this house. She wished she'd been recording. Then again, Helen had always said the same thing. *One enemy at a time.*

Artemis shook her head, avoiding another pile of Jasper's droppings.

She didn't look back. She could hear the jets from the Jacuzzi, the bubble of the hot tub, and the splash of the woman getting out.

As Artemis reached the edge of a garden path, on the other side of a rosebush, she was met by Snake-eyes.

His arms were crossed, and he grunted, nodding back towards the gate.

She didn't need a second invitation.

There were far worse ways this visit into a mobster's mansion could have gone.

Now, her mind was whirring.

Her brother had been telling the truth. At least, the story checked out. The details were the same. A daughter killed, and then three thugs killed afterwards.

Unarmed, though. That was interesting.

What sort of person could kill three men without a weapon?

The answer seemed obvious now. The mental pictures she had taken earlier flashed across her mind of the knot on the handlebars of the jet ski. A special type of knot.

Someone who could fight and kill and tie special knots. Military.

It seemed the best explanation.

But now, she'd had a chance to speak to Sophie herself. It was only as the silver gate began to close behind her, that she realized Sophie wasn't the listed owner of this house.

Jones. That had been the name Forester had provided. An uncle and his nephew.

Artemis shot a look back over her shoulder, frowning at the large mansion.

No movement. Save from the guardhouse.

She shook her head, muttering, and glanced back down the hill.

Most of the police had cleared out now.

She spotted some silhouettes against the lake, others moving amidst the trees, scanning the undergrowth. But most of the vehicles were gone. A couple still remained, parked half on the road and half in the forest.

Darkness was coming quickly; evening escaping, night returning.

She swallowed, picking up her pace and moving hastily down the incline, her feet tapping against the asphalt.

Military. Would that help? She still felt as if the killer had to own a mansion or lake house. Somehow he was keeping track of Robin without being noticed. Somehow, he was keeping track of *them*.

She frowned, glancing one way then the other, a shiver along her shoulders.

She inhaled, shakily pausing, considering her options.

Sophie did not seem involved. She would have to speak to Forester and Wade, to see what they had found, but they had also left the mansion without anyone in cuffs. The other lake home option had been an abandoned house—this was also worth checking out.

But, what if she was missing something?

A new piece of information.

Deadly combat without a weapon. Strange knots. Know-how with vehicles.

She paused; scratched her chin and glanced across the water hesitantly.

How was he watching them?

She thought of her brother's advice about widowmakers; sometimes, the biggest threat required a change in perspective.

In her mind's eye, she pictured that camera on top of the silver gate.

And then, slowly, she tilted her head and looked up.

She was confronted by the night, by a canopy of leaves. By nothing except a skyline, untouched by human hands.

She frowned, turning to look the other way.

What had she been expecting to find? Cameras? A helicopter? She wrinkled her nose. She scanned the sky, looking one way then the other.

No, perhaps not. She sighed, dejectedly, glancing back down and slowly strolling to the bottom of the driveway. She didn't look back.

Once again, her eyes were on the ground.

She wasn't watching where she was going. As she moved across the road, a figure stepped up the path that led to the shore where they had found the body.

She accidentally bumped into the figure. "Sorry," she said quickly.

The large figure grunted, muttering, "Careful, ma'am."

Her eyes flicked up. The person she bumped into glanced over as well.

They both went stiff.

She stared at Ross Dawkins. He didn't look so much like a thumb up close. Now, he looked a bit more like a boulder in a police uniform.

His eyes bugged. He still smelled of cheap beer and cigarettes.

She took a sudden step back.

But reactively, his hand shot out, grabbing her wrist.

He squeezed tight.

She remembered he had done the same thing back outside Ms. Ortega's home on the previous case.

"You!" he said with a snarl.

"Let me go," she snapped.

But he snarled. "Not on your life. *You* did this. You killed my sister! You're under arrest." And then he began dragging her, bodily, yanking so hard she was worried her arm might pop from its socket. He jerked her in the direction of his police car.

She yelled desperately as he pulled.

"Let go, let go!"

But he did not. He kept pulling her, huffing and panting. Sweaty and tired, but his eyes full of hatred.

Another figure was sitting in the waiting police car. The thin, mullet-wearing Merl. Ross' brother.

The man frowned through the windshield, his eyes widened, and he pushed out. Instead of protesting, though, he hurried over, handcuffs emerging.

"Stop!" Artemis screamed. "Let go of me."

But the two cops kept shoving her.

She tried to put up resistance. But two men against one small woman was hardly a fair fight. She tried to stamp on the booted foot of Ross, but he didn't even notice.

Now, her arm was being twisted painfully behind her back.

Merl had grabbed her other side. Her shirt ripped where Ross kept tugging.

"Let go! Let go of me! I didn't do this!"

She felt a flash of sympathy for Tommy. How many times had he been treated like this in their youth? But the flash was replaced by fear and anger.

Suddenly, she heard footsteps. Rapid, thumping footsteps.

"Forester, don't," came Grant's voice.

The footsteps didn't hesitate.

Agent Cameron Forester came hurtling out of the trees like a football player. He tackled Ross around the waist and sent the two of them clattering to the tarmac.

"Get off her!" Forester yelled.

Ross shouted in protest, kicking out, and trying to snap Forester's knee. But the experienced fighter darted back. He started moving towards Merl now. A finger raised, pointing towards the smaller officer. "Let her go," Forester snapped. There was no room for discussion.

Artemis tried to yank her hand away from Ross' brother.

But the small man quickly released his grip, both his hands up, and he backed away. Artemis was breathing heavily, pressing fingers against her ripped sleeve.

As she hyperventilated, she could feel her chest tightening.

It was as if a large hand was squeezing her lungs.

She couldn't breathe. Her legs began to buckle. Dark spots across her eyes.

A panic attack! Shit. What timing.

She dropped to the ground, trying to rise again, but struggling. Her body shook horribly.

18

She could hear quick footsteps as others moved up the shore.

Forester was dropping next to her, eyes wide. "Artemis," he said quickly. "Artemis, it's going to be okay." She noticed how he didn't touch her. His hands hovering near but making no contact. He spoke slowly, soothingly. He even shuffled back a few steps.

She remembered that he had mentioned his mother used to have panic attacks.

She felt a bolt of gratitude to Agent Forester. But she couldn't speak. Every time she tried, the words would come out between panted breaths. But each gasp for air did nothing to satisfy her lungs.

Forester tried to speak, but before he could, Artemis managed to shout a gasping warning.

"Behind!" was all she managed before losing the remnants of air in her lungs.

But Forester only took a second to interpret. He whirled around, sharply, his hand darting to his hip.

But too late. Dawkins already had his own weapon raised. He was pointing it straight at Forester's head. "You assaulted an officer," Ross said, his voice shaking.

His brother, from the direction of the police cruiser, was shouting now. "Ross, let it go. Not here."

But Ross Dawkins was not the type to let something go.

His hands were surprisingly steady where he gripped the weapon and glared over it towards Forester.

"You think you *can*?" Forester said, eyes narrowed. The man's voice didn't shake. And while Ross had steady hands, Forester had a steady voice. He planted his feet firmly, chin out, defiant.

Artemis remembered what he had said. He couldn't feel fear the same way others did.

"She's coming with us," Ross snapped. "She's a prime suspect in a murder investigation. And you are protecting her."

"She's not a suspect, you absolute tool. She's an asset. She's helping. I am sorry about your sister. But I'm going to drown you myself if you don't get that thing out of my face."

Forester jabbed a finger towards the man.

"Some sort of tough guy," Ross spat. A globule of spit darkened the ground. "Is that it? You think you're macho?"

Forester flung out his hands. "Dude, don't be stupid. Put the gun down."

But Ross was nodding now. "You think you're some tough guy. I bet you get off on playing hero. Do you like protecting pretty, little killers? I bet you've been thinking about her, haven't you?"

Forester went quiet now. When he spoke again, there was a growl in his voice. "One rule. Don't psychoanalyze me."

But Ross was beyond redirection. He was shaking his head in contempt. "You do not get to tell me what to do," he said, his voice strained.

"No, but I do," said another monotone voice.

Artemis stared, still hyperventilating, still on the ground, spittle falling from her lips, as she desperately tried to breathe. But past Ross, she saw Agent Desmond Wade with his own gun pressed firmly against Dawkins' neck.

Ross swallowed, licking his lips. "You think that's smart?"

"No, I think it's stupid," said Wade, pushing with his gun against Ross's neck to leave no doubt as to the subject of his comment.

"She's a suspect," snapped Dawkins.

"She's not," said Forester.

Wade, Artemis noticed, did not weigh in.

She was growing somewhat tired of being suspected for a murder she had nothing to do with. She supposed it went right along with the family name. But that didn't make it any easier to swallow.

Desperately, gasping, she tried to steady her nerves. But it was just too difficult.

"Let it go," Merl was still saying. "Ross, damn it. Dad said not to do anything until grandpa told us."

"Shut up, Merl," Ross sneered. His voice was laden with contempt. He now turned his ire towards his brother, slowly lowering his weapon as he did.

In the way of bullies around the world, now that he had lost his upper hand with Forester, he redirected his acerbity. "Call dad! Be useful for a change."

The thin, mullet-wearing brother rolled his eyes, adjusted his glasses, but then pushed back into the car, fiddling with the radio.

Forester pointed at Wade. "Cuff the idiot."

Ross froze. He tried to lift his weapon again, but Wade caught his wrist and squeezed. The weapon hit the ground, clattering.

"Let him go," Agent Grant snapped.

The older woman had finally reached the road. She was panting, breathing heavily. This was the first time she didn't carry an air of extreme competence or authority. Now she just looked winded.

She was wearing two new earrings; these ones looked like pearls.

"Let him go," Grant said. "We don't need trouble. We're trying to solve a case."

Forester yelled, "He threatened to kill me! He tried to arrest Artemis!"

Grant shot Forester a look. "Cameron, let him go."

Forester looked ready to arrest the man himself. But Wade lowered his weapon and stepped back.

Ross, muttering darkly and issuing more than one vitriolic diatribe, stooped to pick up his weapon.

But before he could, Agent Forester kicked.

His foot caught the gun and sent it flying through the air, into the trees, and—a second later—with a faint *plop,* into the lake.

Ross straightened, his face red. His hands tensed.

Forester looked him dead in the eyes. "Advice? You don't want to do it without a gun. No, no, listen. You don't want to do it without a gun. Hear me?"

The two men stared at each other, both breathing heavily, both disheveled from their tussle on the ground.

Wade watched carefully. His gun was holstered now.

Agent Grant was trying to gather her breath, like Artemis, and shaking her head in frustration.

"Just leave," Grant finally said, pointing towards the police cruiser.

Ross pointed at Forester. "I'll get—"

Forester slapped his hand and snapped, "I don't need your threats. Bring five of your best friends and meet me in any alley. I look forward to it."

Ross spat again. And then, muttering, cursing, and threatening, he moved with as much dignity as he could salvage towards his waiting brother.

The doors slammed, the headlights flashed.

Wade suddenly yelled, "Get out of the road!"

Forester yanked Artemis to the side, and the vehicle narrowly missed, speeding past them, tires squealing.

She stared after the angry brake lights as they turned around the lakeside road.

"Imbeciles," Grant muttered.

Artemis wasn't sure who she was referring to.

Now, as the car left and she inhaled slowly, Artemis rose, rehearsing one of her favorite tournament games in her mind. It was the first time she had managed to win in under eight moves.

Slowly, as the game played out in her mind, she was able to relax. To breathe a bit easier. And then, her shoulder aching from all the tugging and pulling, she was able to push back to her feet, dusting herself off sheepishly.

It was night, and she remembered she still had that appointment with the Washingtons to go over the postcards. But now, swallowing and glancing at the figures around her, she said, "I think our killer is military."

Grant cut in. "No, wait. Forester, you were out of line."

Forester glared at his aunt. "Are you joking? That idiot was going to break her arm. She's not even a suspect."

Grant shook her head severely. "She's not *our* suspect, yet." She tried to say that last word quickly, as if it were nothing very important.

But to Artemis, it was the loudest and most notable.

Grant continued quickly, "But they're investigating the case as well. You have to give them some latitude. His sister is dead."

Forester shook his head in frustration. "He would have beaten Artemis. You saw that guy."

Grant shook her head, and her finger joined the motion. "You don't know that. And you don't get to infer based on some weird, macho bullshit."

Wade didn't seem to be paying attention. He was still watching Artemis after her *military* comment.

Artemis looked towards Grant then Forester. "I'm sorry," she said. Though she didn't really know what she was apologizing for.

"It's not your fault," Forester insisted, firmly.

"You should get some sleep," Grant returned, her voice cold. "Before you make a mistake. Some of your methods are unconventional, Cameron. But direct insubordination? Not a chance in hell I let you get away with that. You're going to apologize to the Dawkins. In person, first thing tomorrow."

"Like hell I will."

"Forester, try to see the big picture. Women are dying."

Forester pointed at Artemis. "She's a woman. Do we get to care about her?"

"I didn't think you cared about anyone. Isn't that what you told me?"

A silence hung over the road. Everyone was tense, tired. Everyone was angry. Another woman dead.

Hoping to redirect the conversation before people said things they couldn't take back, Artemis said, "I—I, er, spoke to the woman at the mansion. She confirmed my brother's story."

Three sets of eyes turned towards her.

Taking this as a promising start, Artemis continued. "She said a guy named Raul Guillermo lost his daughter three days ago. The same killer took out three of his men, unarmed. Like I said, I think he's military. I also saw–"

"The knot," Wade said.

She looked at him, surprised.

Wade nodded. "Navy," he said.

Grant looked over. "You're sure?"

"It's not one of ours," said Wade with a shrug. "They used a clove hitch. Green Berets prefer a prusik knot."

Artemis blinked in surprise. She hadn't realized Wade was ex-military.

"So how does that help us?" Grant said firmly.

"I can call the families," Wade replied. "The Dawkins might speak with me and I don't think they'll recognize my voice."

"Good," Grant said quickly, nodding. "Ask about family connections with military background."

"We still haven't identified the girl we found," Artemis cut in.

But Forester shook his head. "We did."

"Oh? What's her name?"

"Judy Holdsworth."

Artemis wrinkled her nose. "I don't recognize that name."

Forester said, "You wouldn't. She's here visiting her father. He only just moved a couple of years ago."

"What do we know about her?"

"Not much," Grant said. "Which is why, Wade, you will speak to the family. If not tonight, first thing tomorrow. And Forester, I'm serious, you will apologize in person to Dawkins, or you're out. And

Wade, you can drive me to the hotel." Jerking a finger at Forrester and Artemis, she spat, "You two can get a damn taxi."

And with that, her voice shaking with emotion and frustration, Agent Grant marched away, and Wade, wincing apologetically, followed.

Artemis stared towards the sedan as Grant slammed the front door and Wade slipped into the driver's seat.

"That's our ride," Artemis said, her voice weak.

Forester was still glaring, his lips pressed tight, his hands clenched into fists.

"Forget about her," he muttered. "I'll call a taxi. You okay?"

Artemis let out a shaky breath. "Maybe," she said, weakly, "is there a way to look at homeowners with a military background?"

Forester was pulling his phone out, clearly distracted. She repeated the question, a bit louder this time.

He glanced at her and shrugged. "Should be easy enough. Yeah. Are you staying at a hotel?"

Artemis nodded. "There's only one in Pinelake."

"Right. I guess I better get a room there too."

For some reason, this made her uncomfortable. But it wasn't like she could protest. Instead, inhaling slowly, gathering air as if it might be the last breath she could take, she said, "Thank you. I'm sorry I got you in trouble."

Forester shook his head. "Bureaucracy got me in trouble. It's not your fault. You sure you're okay?"

She wasn't used to this much concern, or anger, from Forester. Normally he was making wisecracks or putting her in dangerous situations.

And again, she felt distinctly uncomfortable.

"I'm fine," she said. "Maybe I should get my own taxi."

"What, why?"

Artemis realized the reason wasn't one she could say out loud. She didn't want to sit in a car with him. She didn't want to go to a hotel with him. She wasn't sure where the sudden discomfort was coming from. But she knew, with certainty, she wanted to drive alone. But this, she decided, would be impossible to suggest without offending him. So in the end, she just shook her head and muttered. "No, never mind. Sorry."

But Forester was no longer paying attention, still distracted and scowling and speaking already to someone on the phone.

Night had stretched, but it seemed strange to take a break, to call it quits for the day.

Then again, maybe a little bit of regrouping was what they needed.

Artemis winced, her wrist throbbing—most likely bruised. Again, she glanced up, eyes on the sky. Her gaze tracked the blinking stars, the faint glow of the moon.

How was the killer watching them? Watching his victims?

She frowned now, determined that one way or another, she would find out.

19

He stood by the desk, frowning at the image on the computer. He leaned in, wrinkling his nose and studying the familiar face.

"I know you," he murmured slowly.

She had dark hair pulled back in a simple ponytail. Wore a plain, long-sleeved fleece and dark pants. No piercings, no makeup—pretty, in an unassuming sort of way. In the image, a faint tinge of red crept across her face. He didn't blame her, though—she'd been the one to find the third body. He could remember how it felt attaching it to the jet ski...

Some might suggest he was putting too fine a point on it, but he knew Pinelake. Certain sorts could be dense unless a message was written in big letters across the sky.

This was his version of writing in big letters.

He glanced back at the image of the woman he'd taken. He bit his lip, and then his eyes widened. He remembered now... exactly where he'd read about her. He leaned his large forearm against the desk, and then typed on his keyboard, opening the local news station's digital archives.

It had been ten years ago, hadn't it? No... nothing there.

More? Ah—there it was. Fifteen years ago, then.

He opened the article and there she was. Standing outside an old, two-story home, tears streaming from those strange, mismatched eyes. The article's title read, *Ghostkiller's Daughter Leads to His Capture...*

He didn't read the article. Didn't need to.

She wasn't as young as the other victims had been. But she fit what he was looking for. He nodded slowly, feeling a faint tremor of delight.

Yes... yes, she'd do perfectly.

As he stared at the news article open on his screen, his mind flitted back to another article. He swallowed now, feeling his skin prickle, his temper starting to spark.

The woodsman didn't like coming into the office, zombie-like at his standing desk. But now, as he stared at the image on the screen, he could feel his heart skipping in his chest. His vision narrowed...

He read the article's headline again.

Other headlines flashed through his mind. Not long ago. Not fifteen years ago.

The news could be downright cruel, at times. But he'd always known this.

And so he'd grown cruel, too.

He released a faint rumbling growl in his throat, staring at the computer. It was getting late now. He was the only one in the office.

Not that it would have mattered.

Yes... yes, she would be next.

It wasn't fair, they all got to live. Wasn't fair, *she* had died but they survived. No—no, he could remember *years* of mockery. Years of their whispers and taunts. Remembered reading the comments on the article. People he'd known. People he'd gotten drinks with.

No... No, this wasn't over.

This wouldn't be over until Pinelake was drowned in the tears of mourning. Until the lake itself was overflowing with the dead.

He slammed a hand against the screen.

Except sometimes, he forgot his own strength.

His fist cracked the monitor, sending the device off the standing desk and crashing to the ground. He snorted, staring at it.

He didn't bother to pick it up. Instead, he turned, snatched at his briefcase of supplies along with the wheeled box he used for work, and he began to stalk back through the office building. Night, visible through the windows. Everyone else was now home... with their families.

His teeth pressed tightly, and he snarled as he picked up the pace, listening to the faint whir of wheels against carpet as he marched towards the exit.

He glanced down at his suitcase and paused to poke the small piece of wire jutting past the zipper. He pushed the wire back in, zipped up the compartment, and picked up the pace, his anticipation mounting.

It wouldn't be hard to find where Artemis Blythe was staying.

There was only one hotel in town, after all.

20

"Wʜᴀᴛ ᴡᴀs ᴛʜᴇ ɢɪʀʟ's name again?" asked Mrs. Washington, her nose wrinkling where she sat snug in a quilt she'd knitted. Her husband was busy with a small, wooden clock, frowning as he tried to get the thing to start working again.

Artemis also sat beneath her covers. But the hotel bed was far less comfortable than her analysts' setup. She frowned at the grainy image on the computer screen as it began to stutter and skip. The hotel, the *Seasonal Comfort Delux* with the 'e' intentionally missing, according to the owner, wasn't exactly known for its high-speed internet.

Again, Artemis found herself missing her small apartment back in Salinas. A small, terrified part of her was beginning to wonder if she'd ever make it back.

"Judy Holdsworth," Artemis said. "Why?"

"Because... I think I found her," said Cynthia, tapping Henry on the arm. "Henry—what's that there?"

217

He looked over, scowling. "Where are your reading glasses, woman?"

She paused, frowning one way then other. Artemis paused long enough so she wouldn't offend them then cleared her throat. Henry was still scowling at his cuckoo clock, but Cynthia looked up in time to see Artemis pointing at her hair.

The older woman's hand darted up, paused, and then her eyes widened in relief. She removed her glasses from where they'd been pushed up on her head, adjusted them and leaned in. A bit *too* close to the screen—half her face now blocked the webcam.

But then she leaned back a second later. "Yes—yes, I found her here. There's an article in the paper about her."

Artemis frowned. She was thinking through the other victims so far. Robin the daughter of a policeman. This mafioso's daughter. Was the killer targeting people involved with the judicial system?"

"Let me guess," Artemis said. "Her father or mother is a judge or a lawyer or something."

Henry looked up now too, peering down his long nose. But then he brightened. "Ha!" he crowed. "I never thought I'd see the day."

"Slow down, speedy," his wife said, elbowing him beneath the blanket. "Not all of us are speed-readers."

"Wait, what is it, Mr. Washington?" Artemis said.

"Oh, nothing," he chortled. "I'm just enjoying this one moment when Artemis Blythe happens to be wrong."

She paused then leaned back in her hotel room bed. Occasionally, her eyes darted to the locks on the door. She'd bolted it too. Forester had a room on the floor below. And yet, even more than during the car ride back to the hotel, Artemis still felt a strange sense of discomfort. Flustered as she'd been, she'd even forgotten to bring up Forester's comments from earlier.

She shook her head, refocusing. "No lawyer? No judge?"

"What about a clerk or a prison guard or something?" Cynthia added, still slowly reading the article online while continually adjusting her glasses.

"Nope," said Henry. He opened his mouth to reply, but his wife must have reached the relevant part now too.

She cut in with, "Oh, I see! Her parents work in pharmaceuticals—it mentions it at the bottom of the paragraph."

Artemis wrinkled her nose. "So what... what was Holdsworth in the paper for? When's it from?"

"Looks like... last year."

"Can you send it to me?"

No sooner had she said it, than a small speech bubble appeared in the bottom corner of her screen. She clicked the link and it led to a page with the title. "*Small Town Whiz Wins Varsity Science Fair.*"

Artemis stared, shaking her head and leaning back. "That... doesn't make sense," she said. "So the parents aren't involved at all?"

The Washingtons watched their screen. Henry had lowered his clock. "Can we drop the nasty business?" he asked. "I thought you wanted to go over this cipher?"

Artemis shook her head in frustration, trying to figure out exactly what she was missing. But then she nodded and said, "Of course, sorry, sir. Did you find anything yet?"

"Yes," he said. "There is no cipher."

Artemis frowned. "How can you be sure?"

"I'm *not* sure. But I've looked at it for three hours now since you sent it. There's *nothing*. No acrostics, no number replacement, no alphabet shift... nothing." He glanced at his wife who had hooked her arm through his. She was shaking her head as well. "Sorry, Artemis. I didn't find anything either," she said.

Artemis sighed. "It's fine. Thanks for looking, at least. I... I don't get it." Then, she quickly added. "And thanks for humoring me with the other stuff. I'm sorry—it's grim."

"So you say they want you to *consult*?" Henry asked. "They're paying you, aren't they? They better be."

"I was told yes," said Artemis. "But I'm not sure."

"You're a good woman," said Cynthia, nodding firmly, her dark features wrinkling around her eyes as she smiled. "You're doing the right thing. Just... don't forget..." she shifted her glasses back onto her forehead. "Nationals, remember?"

"I remember. I know," Artemis said quickly. "I'll be studying. It... hopefully, I'll have a chance soon."

She shrugged uncomfortably. As she did, though, she frowned. "Cy nthia... where did you see that article about Judy?"

"Oh—umm... It's a small news website in your town. IB-News, looks like."

Artemis paused, wrinkling her nose. "Do..." Then, instead of finishing the question, she began typing hurriedly herself. She scanned the IB-News front page for a search bar, then her fingers flew across the keys as she typed in *Judy Holdsworth.*

An article popped up. The same science-fair article Cynthia had found.

"What is it?" Ms. Washington was saying, studying her screen. "Is everything alright?"

Artemis was biting her lip now and nodded quickly. She didn't reply, but instead was now pausing, her fingers hovering over the keyboard. A mobster's daughter... A cop's daughter... A mobster... a cop... a science fair...

Artemis' eyes widened. She'd been too distracted with those damn postcards. The real pattern was staring her in the face. She typed in *Raul Guillermo.* The name of the mobster. A couple of articles came up.

But one in particular stood out. In between the others. She frowned, staring at it. The article's title read... *Princess to a Criminal Empire Speaks Out.*

She clicked the link, scanning it quickly. The article described the way *Raul Guillermo's* only daughter, Camilla, had hosted a sit-in protest for an animal rights activity at her university. Artemis scanned the article, ignoring most of it. She frowned, shaking her head, and then searched the same website a second time.

This time, she entered *Robin Dawkins*.

There were quite a few articles now, almost six pages of results. Most of them due to the last name. Some read things like, *Local Sheriff Honored by Library.* Or *Shooting Last Night Stopped by Hero Cop.* As she skipped from page to page, other articles read things like. *Internal Investigation Into Beat Cop's Bullying Ways...*

But there, on the very last page...

Robin Dawkins, Local Champion!

Artemis clicked the link, staring. She could hear the Washingtons still attempting to gain her attention over the computer speakers.

But now prickles spread across her skin. She consciously closed the tab with the postcards opened, forcing her mind to focus. Her eyes skipped along the web page, quickly reading. It was from two years ago. Some track and field success story.

"Holy..." Artemis bit her lip.

"What is it?" Cynthia was saying. "Artemis, are you alright?"

But she was pushing to her feet now. Her skin prickled. She flashed a quick smile to the Washingtons. "Thank you—thank you so much for your help. But I have to go!"

"Artemis!" Henry said. "Hang on, is everything alright?"

Artemis flashed a thumbs up. "Fine... fine, I think I know how he's targeting them."

The Washingtons looked confused, and she wanted nothing more than to linger, speaking to them well into the night. It was getting late. Nearly ten PM now, according to the clock on her computer.

But she needed to hurry.

Forester was in a room on the floor below. He had to see this. Her breath came quickly, her pulse racing. She gave a final farewell to the Washingtons and then shut the laptop in a rush. She double-checked she had her phone, the room key, and then she hastened towards the door, practically jogging.

Her eyes were wide, her skin still prickling. She shoved through the door and shut it quickly.

She nearly yelped as a shadow moved out of the corner of her eye.

Her heart pounded, but she realized, a second later, it was just one of the hotel employees checking an ice machine. She smiled at the man, quickly—he didn't even look at her—and she then hastened to the stairs, taking them two at a time.

She was winded by the time she reached the bottom.

Shit. She thought, gasping. She needed to make sure she kept in better shape for moments like these. So much of her time, in recent months, had been spent preparing for the upcoming tournaments that she'd struggled to keep her morning jogging routine.

Now, though, cursing her lack of lung capacity, she hastened towards Forester's room. C1—that's what the clerk had said, wasn't it?

She paused, closing her eyes and casting back to the moment Forester had received his keycard. She watched the image play out like a movie. Then she nodded quickly. C1. Coincidentally, one of the worst opening moves in chess.

She hastened to the door to Forester's room, knuckles pounding the frame.

"Forester!" she whispered. "Cameron! Hey!" She knocked a bit louder.

She heard shuffling from inside, and only then did she realize she was wearing her thin t-shirt. Her sweater was back in the room. She felt cold all of a sudden, exposed. Even her hair was now loose as she'd removed the hairband and placed it next to her bed. She wasn't even wearing shoes.

Dammit.

She'd been too excited to show him.

For a moment, she half turned, wanting to race back and put on another layer - grab shoes and to do her hair. No sense in giving the agent the wrong impres—

The door opened. A tall man with bed-head stared out at her. He blinked, holding his scarred hand to stifle a yawn. She paused now, staring, wide-eyed. He so often wore mis-buttoned suits and long sleeves, she'd never quite seen the extent of his wounded arm.

A scar roped up from his palm, along his arm, twisting up to his shoulder.

He wasn't wearing a shirt, and she'd underestimated just how defined Forester was. His muscles weren't thick, but they were readily apparent. A strong physique, even a six pack. But her eyes saw the scar moving from his belly up towards his collarbone, nearly intersecting with the second scar down his arm.

She swallowed, feeling a flush of horror at the gruesome wound.

Forester noted where she stood, yawned and nodded once. "Couldn't resist my charm, I see."

She didn't even respond to the jibe. Instead, she stared at his chest. "Are... are you okay?"

He shrugged, leaning against the door. No hint of embarrassment whatsoever. For a moment, Artemis wondered what that must feel like. A complete and casual indifference to the opinions of others. She wasn't sure if she was more envious or terrified by the prospect.

"I mean... not *exactly* what a man wants to hear from a hot chick," Forester replied. "But yeah. I'm okay."

Artemis frowned at him. "Stop that, please."

"Stop what?"

"Saying that. You've said it three times now. It's rude."

"What's rude?"

She glared. "Stop calling me *that.*"

He watched her, his eyes mischievous. "Calling you *what*?" he said.

Now, she realized he was just teasing, and she wanted to kick him for it. She realized a lot of her emotions towards Forester verged on a desire for physical and immediate violence. For a moment, she almost forgot why she'd come down.

"Stop commenting on my appearance," Artemis at last said primly, trying to remain focused. "It's inappropriate."

Forester pointed at her. "You just commented on mine."

"I asked if you were *okay*! That's different. You're not wearing a shirt!"

"See—you did it again."

She was beginning to grow flustered now. How could one man be so infuriating? It was as if he *wanted* to test her blood pressure. She said, firmly this time. "Stop commenting on my appearance. I mean it."

Forester looked at her, considering it. "You really mean it?"

"Yes!" she exclaimed, exasperated. But then, she thought she heard movement from the room next door, and she whispered again. "Yes! Why wouldn't I? Most work environments would call it harassment, Cameron."

"Huh. I thought I was complimenting you."

She shook her head, hands tensed. She wasn't sure exactly how to interact with this man. But at least he seemed willing to listen. Carefully, as if speaking to a child, she said, "It isn't appropriate to comment on someone's physical appearance in a work environment. I hope you understand. I could report you to HR."

He blinked at her. Up until this last part, Forester seemed to have been softening to her rebuke. But the moment she said *HR*, his eyes narrowed. "I get it now. You want to kiss, is that it? Alright then—you first." He waggled his eyebrows at her.

Artemis was torn now. She mostly wanted to stomp away. But on the other hand, she *did* have something the insufferable man needed to see. "I'm going to tell Grant," she said at last, with a firm nod.

Forester instantly looked a lot less coy. "Wait, hang on—let's talk about it."

"No. I'm telling. The world is not your playpen, Cameron." Her eyes darted back towards his scars. But worried he might misinterpret the glance, she shook her head, quickly fishing her phone from her pocket. "That aside," she said firmly, still refusing to give him space to be his usual self and make a smartass remark, "I found something."

Forester sobered a bit now. The tall sociopath frowned, crossing his muscled and scarred arms. "On the case?"

"Yes!" she said excitedly, some of her anger filtering away. "Look!"

She pulled her phone out, cycling to the same website and hastily entering the names of the articles she'd memorized. She turned her phone, showing it to Forester.

He wrinkled his nose, leaning in. He swiped on the phone, scanning from one article to the next. "Holy shit..." he murmured. "Killer is targeting..."

"Girls in the news," Artemis said. "But... but I don't know if it's *just* that. I ran through the articles on my way down here—"

"On the stairs?"

"Yes! But I was noticing—"

"You read all three articles on the stairs?"

"No—I ran through them!" she said exasperated. "I played them in my mind."

"What... like a memory trick?"

"Something like that. Look that's not important. I noticed *two* things in commonality. Forester, each article mentions the girls' fathers alongside some achievement the girls made. They're also all stories from Pinelake. I don't know exactly *why* he's targeting them, but I know he's picking women from Pinelake whose fathers are also mentioned in the news."

Forester wrinkled his nose. "What the hell? Why?"

And then Artemis nearly dropped her phone. She glanced up, noticing a small security camera in the hallway of the hotel. Tastefully concealed in a black, glass orb, near one of the sprinklers.

"The... the news van," she said slowly.

"What's that?"

"The IB-News van outside the barn," she murmured. "They arrived at the same time as the police."

"So?"

"So Wade thought it was because the police notified the news crew. But *why* would the sheriff do that at first if his own granddaughter was the victim? He wouldn't want looky-loos on site right away, would he?"

"What's your point?"

Artemis was taking her phone back now with shaking hands. She hastily cycled through the website to the more recent news. And then she spotted the article about the murder from the morning. Her hands shook, she swallowed. A single photo of the barn and the lake. The caption next to the photo read *Sheriff's Daughter Murdered.*

But it was the photo she was interested in. She stared, voice shaking as she said, "Look at this." She turned her device.

21

Forester glanced down at the phone. "What about it?"

"The photograph. Look at it."

"Umm... I mean, I guess I see the lake... the people in the barn... I see some blockade... That *might* be the body? Can't be sure. Not a high-quality image..."

"No... no but look at the angle."

Forester hesitated, then shrugged. "High up. They must have used a drone or something. Lot of news crews are—"

"A drone! Forester—get it? That's how he's been watching us. That's how he's known the girls' routines without alarming them. He doesn't own a house on the lake. He's using a drone to track them." Artemis could feel her blood pumping, watched the way Forester's eyes suddenly widened in shock. Then, her voice hoarse, she added. "And...

and that's how the news crew was there at the same time as the police. No one told them, Forester. They knew about the murder *before*."

"Wait... *what*? You think a *news* crew is—"

"No—not all of them! Just... this guy!" She pointed towards the picture on the article. "The drone pilot. I—I think I saw him in the IB-News van." She thought back desperately, her heart still skipping, her skin still prickling. She nodded hurriedly. "Yes—yes, I did! Someone was sitting in the front seat, their breath fogging the glass. A cameraman was arguing with a cop. A woman was standing under an umbrella. But the man *in* the van. He was probably piloting the drone. The rain had nearly stopped. It's him! It's..." She leaned in now, staring at the picture and reading the photo credit beneath.

Carter Sowell.

"Carter Sowell," she murmured. She wrinkled her nose.

"Slow your roll, Artemis. Why? Why is some news guy popping young women—"

She knew. In that moment, Artemis *knew* she knew. She didn't reply but instead, started typing furiously on her phone, her fingers flying over the keyboard. *Carter Sowell.*

She entered the name in the search bar of the website. A few articles showed up. Many of them displaying photos that Carter had captured.

But one... the very earliest one, from nearly six years ago, caught her attention.

The article title read: *Ex-SEAL's Daughter Drowns—Daddy Helpless.*

Her eyes widened. Forester, noting her reaction, stepped in the hall, staring over her shoulder at the phone. The two of them read in silence. Artemis murmured. "God... It's him. It's *him!*"

Forester was also staring, stunned. He read quietly, *"...SEAL asleep pontooning on Pine Lake. Daughter trapped under boat..."* He kept skimming, reading portions. *"...Embarrassing negligence... What type of father? Disgrace to the uniform..."*

"Shit," Artemis whispered. "His own daughter drowned."

"Look here," Forester said, as if mesmerized. "He only dozed off for about three minutes. They had thrown the anchor. The man's wife was on the boat too, but she was talking to a friend. Shit." Forester shook his head, looking sick. "The girl drowned without her parents even knowing. She tried to swim from one side of the pontoon to the other but got trapped... because of a white boat-cover caught under the boat..." Forester pointed at another picture. "Look at that fabric—that's... that's *almost* the same material used..."

"The gowns the girls wear... It's woven from the same fabric," Artemis whispered... Her eyes moved to another portion of the article. "Three minutes," Artemis whispered. "He was only asleep for a few minutes, but she drowned..." She felt a faint lump in her throat. She still couldn't quite figure out how to summon tears. She hadn't cried in nearly a decade and a half.

But she couldn't imagine the anguish.

"He got a job with them?" she said, stunned. "After they wrote an article like this? He worked for them?"

"Yeah—look here. Three years later," Forester said, tapping the phone over her shoulder, his scarred and calloused hand grazing her cheek as he fiddled with the buttons. "*IB-News Welcomes New Member to Aerial Camera Crew.*" He was nodding. "No mention of the article. No apology. Nothing. But you're right. He's a damn drone pilot. And an ex-Navy SEAL. Holy shit. Imagine that? A SEAL's daughter drowning."

"Is that... worse than anyone else?" Artemis said, frowning.

"Hell yeah. Those guys call themselves frogmen. They take the water very seriously." Forester was shaking his head, his eyes wide. "Alright—well, way to go, Checkers. I'll call Wade and Grant. Wade was going to set up an interview with Ms. Holdsworth's family. But no point now. Here, let me get dressed—you grab some shoes. Actually, no," he shook his head. "What am I thinking—you're not even an agent. Go hide in your room. We got it from here."

Artemis didn't protest this time. The last couple of times she'd gone with the agents to the crime scenes, it hadn't ended well. She wanted no more run-ins with angry cops or ex-cons. Perhaps the Washingtons would still be up.

She felt a surge of elation as she turned on her heel. Forester was slipping back into his room. She shot a look over her shoulder and grinned. "Good luck," she whispered.

He winked and shut the door.

Her feeling of elation accompanied her as she moved back up the stairs, hurrying to her room. She couldn't help but smile.

She'd found the killer. She was nearly certain this was their guy. Yes... yes, she'd *done* it.

She gave a little fist pump as she reached the second floor, but quickly cleared her throat and dropped the gesture, even though no one was watching. The man checking the ice machine was gone too. The doors closed. The dark hall stretching before her as she pulled her keycard from her pocket.

She felt a faint jolt of discomfort and wrinkled her nose. Good thing she hadn't been in Pinelake recently. She knew at least one article that mentioned her chess success and her father's name in the IB-News archives. Perhaps it *was* best to just hunker down.

Still... Her keycard in hand, she paused outside her door, frowning.

There were implications to this. Implications to solving the case... It felt... almost like winning a tournament. The same elation, the same delight.

But more than that...

Lives would be saved. Men like this... killers like this... like her father—they thrived because they weren't caught. They killed. Sometimes for years. Sometimes decades.

But she'd already caught two, hadn't she?

She bit her lip. She needed to study for the national tournament next month.

But what if...

"No, no," she muttered to herself, shaking her head. "Don't be silly." She slipped her keycard into the slot. The light above the handle turned green.

But she paused again, frowning, and thinking. She already knew she could ace the strategic competency portion of the FBI field test. She'd done so three years ago as part of a PR move by her then-manager.

Would it really be so bad to just... *try* some basic field training? But why? It wasn't like she'd ever work with them again. She'd been forced into it twice now. This *wasn't* what she wanted to do.

What about Helen?

A small voice whispered in her mind.

It was this thought that stopped her cold. Hand half-turning the door handle. Helen... was she still alive? Her father kept insisting it. What if some other man had kidnapped her sister? What if Helen was still out there?

One enemy at a time. But... but if Artemis had to *choose* an enemy. It would be the bastard who hurt her sister.

She'd always thought the Ghostkiller, her old man, was responsible. But what if the victims he'd chosen had been a *reaction* to his daughter going missing? What if something had broken in grief...

That's what had happened here, wasn't it? A father had lost his own daughter.

And so he'd killed others...

It didn't make sense to Artemis... But to these sorts of minds...

She pushed the door slowly open, feeling shivers and prickles. What if Helen really was alive? Training with the FBI, consulting with them, would give her avenues and resources she'd never have otherwise to locate her sister.

"Just because dad didn't kill her, doesn't mean she's alive," Artemis murmured to herself.

This, she knew was true... Seventeen years ago, Helen had disappeared. Seventeen years was a very, very long time. She was probably dead anyway.

Artemis bit her lip.

But what if not?

What if there was a chance?

She let out a faint breath. The exhilaration was gone... but something else, something more rigid and cold had replaced it. A certainty. A determination.

She stepped into her hotel room and caught a gust of cool air.

She paused, frowning as the door slowly swung shut behind her.

Then, her eyes landed on the window. She hadn't left it open... It wasn't even a question. She *knew* she hadn't left it open. She memorized the layout of her hotel room. So why was the window wide open? The drapes fluttering?

She must have entered the wrong room. She shook her head in confusion, turning towards the door to leave.

But no... her laptop on the bed. Her sweater by the dresser. Her shoes by the—

A large shadow suddenly arose from behind the bed. A massive, dark figure.

Her heart nearly leapt from her chest. She gaped at the man, loosed a small squeak. She felt a flare of anxiety blossom to panic in her gut.

And then he came charging right at her, leaping the entire bed in one gigantic stride.

22

Artemis tried to scream, but her lungs had emptied—the anxiety knot turning to full blown panic in an instant. The same as when she'd collapsed on the lake-side road, her knees nearly buckled.

But *he* didn't have any such hesitation. He moved *impossibly* fast. In fact, he was *impossibly* big. At least seven foot. His hand slammed over her mouth. His arm was corded with muscle, his eyes blazing in fury. Tattoos patterned up the giant's skin. His face was strangely wet, as if he'd recently been in a shower, his thin-cut hair plastered to his forehead.

"Three minutes," he whispered beneath his breath, hand holding her firm against the door. "That's how long—you get three minutes."

And then he pulled, with one straining arm, the entire *bed* to block the door. He slipped past and began to drag her towards the bathroom. The physical motion, the sharp pain jolted her, somewhat. Her anxiety continued to swirl, to pulse, but she was able to move. She resisted with all her might, trying to scream, but the sweaty hand kept her lips sealed. Trying to kick, but where her bare feet struck the giant's massive shins, they only rebounded. She struggled desperately, attempting to bite his fingers now. But his hand encased half her head, his other hand suddenly dipped under her and lifted her, his forearm like a beam of iron against her belly.

He carried her as if she were little more than a rag doll towards the door to the bathroom. He kicked the door open, still stopping her screams. She was caught between emotional panic and physically crippling terror.

And then she spotted the sink. It was full of water. Some of it having sloshed on the floor. Her eyes wide, full of horror, she couldn't quite understand what she was staring at. He reached the tub, though, using a foot to kick a faucet. He then used the same foot to knock a plug into the bath drain.

The water began to run, making a shushing sound where it splashed into the curve of the porcelain.

"Three minutes," he whispered. "That's what it takes... Three minutes too late, and you're a coward. An embarrassment. A mockery!" He kept her hefted over one shoulder, but the awkward grip now caused her mouth to slip free.

She inhaled deeply, her lungs only *just* working, and tried to scream, "Fore—"

But he caught her again, this time shoving her against the tiled wall and holding her up by the neck. His fingers were like metal rebar wrapped around her throat, holding her fast. Her feet kicked, and only now did she realize just how big the giant was.

Even dangling a good foot off the ground , he was still taller than her.

He was wider than the sink. A giant, muscled, wall of a man. His breath smelled faintly of alcohol, his eyes fixed on her, a bright green. "Your father isn't any better... He isn't! No—no, but I'm the one." He sneered now, his voice competing for dominance with the sound of the running water. "I'm the one who is mocked. A disgrace to my uniform! That's what they said. They printed it. A failure... Negligent..." He shook his head, chuckling now. There was no humor to his voice, though. "How come you get to live, huh? How come?"

Artemis could see the madness in the man's warped gaze. She couldn't breathe though, her throat constricted. Desperately, she tried to *think*. Forester was a fighter, but this man... this man was a trained killer. He'd murdered three mobsters who'd gone after him. Even as her air failed her, as she struggled for breath, her mind was swimming rapidly, desperately.

No time... There was no time to get Forester... Not unless...

She was struggling desperately now — gasping for air. The water was starting to fill up past the edge of the tub. She watched where it sloshed over the porcelain and began to spill along the tiled floor, spreading in a glaze.

The giant continued to squeeze her throat, shaking his head in fury. "You don't get to live—if she dies, you die!" he roared. "They call *me* negligent? Hmm? Where's your father? Where is he, Artemis? Where!"

She didn't have the air to respond. She could only think of one option. He'd barricaded the door with the entire damn bed. There was no way help could come that way. The window?

No time... No time to communicate.

Her fingers were scrambling desperately in her pocket—she needed to buy time. She managed to click the phone. She could hear it faintly dialing, connecting. She couldn't let *him* hear though.

So she began to try and speak, her voice strangled, strained.

"P-please..." she tried.

But he didn't seem to care. Her back was pressed to the wall, but the towel rack was next to her. The moment the phone connected, though, Forester would speak. It would alert the monster. So she desperately scrambled for the buttons on the side. Her fingers were dexterous from years of time management, moving pieces. But it took her, with trembling hands, far too long to mute the volume. Now that the tub was full, he finally seemed to notice.

"Ha!" he said. "Three minutes." And then he pulled her from the wall.

No time to think. She left her phone wedged against the towel draped over the rack. She got a final glimpse of the device. A video call—she hadn't even managed a normal call.

Shit... would Forester even answer?

She couldn't see.

She tried to protest. "Wait—please—"

Too late. He jammed her head under the water, holding her there. She struggled desperately, kicking, scratching. But he was too damn strong.

She wondered if she ought to fake dead. But no...

She tried to think. But there was so much fear... so much panic. She reached back with her arms, but it was like trying to wrestle an iron beam. Her fingers strained, both hands useless behind her back. Air bubbles scampered past her cheeks. The tub was cold. Very cold. The water nipping and swishing and splashing.

Her shirt was soaked where she was pressed. She could feel his legs behind her, like tree roots, absolutely unmoving.

Think... Think... Think!

All she had was her mind. He was far too strong. No weapon, no training. Just her mind...

She remembered Helen, years ago... sometimes one could be *too* clever. The obvious answer was the *right* answer.

Artemis hesitated. Her eyes strained in the water, in pain. She couldn't breathe, could barely see. But her hands were free.

Suddenly, it struck her.

How long had she been under? How long did she have left?

She reached out, desperate, and pulled the plug.

She could hear the water starting to drain. Could hear the way it swirled and sucked back into the drain. She was careful to keep her hand under water, out of sight, desperately—so very desperately—gripping the plug so he wouldn't realize what she'd done.

How long to drain a bathtub halfway? One minute? Two...

She couldn't breathe, her lungs protested. Bubbles continued to sail past her cheeks. She tried to play dead now. Going motionless, rigid, draped into the tub.

But he didn't seem to care.

Three minutes...

That's how long he'd been asleep without realizing what was happening to his daughter. The length of a song? How had he managed to track it?

Strange questions. She didn't have the answers.

Not that it mattered. She could *feel* the water level slowly lowering. It was only a brief moment. The door was blockaded. The window was open, but why would Forester think to use the window?

The water level continued to fall. She tried her best to play dead. It wasn't like she could even make a sound.

The giant of a man was speaking above her, but his words were muted by the liquid. His iron grip, completely unrelenting.

Her eyes stung, her nostrils stung. No more air. The water, though, was still lowering. He must have noticed now. Must have...

"Hey, wait... you little bitch!" he roared.

Yes. He'd noticed. Plus, she could hear him now. The water was now down to her cheeks.

Black spots across her eyes. Her mind loopy—as if half-drunk. The pain in her lungs was terrifyingly immense.

But then...

The water swished past her lips. She gasped, desperate. Grateful for a brief respite. She felt a slap across the back of her head from a hand the size of a baseball mitt. She blacked out instantly.

She came to a second later, realizing now he was ripping the plug from her fingers.

"Think you're clever?" he screamed over her. "Three minutes. That's the deal, bitch. You don't get less—you think you're special? Your daddy is special? Hmm? I'll show you special." He lifted her, dragging her sopping wet, water pouring in rivulets, and shoved her face towards the sink now.

She didn't have much time to breathe. This time, she doubted he'd let her reach the plug.

Suddenly, though, she heard loud pounding.

"Open up, FBI!" A screaming, desperate voice. Forester.

The pounding wasn't knocking. It sounded like he was kicking the door. She heard gunshots. Shooting the lock? But an entire bed was blocking the door.

She had a brief choice. Needed the air in her lungs. But Forester needed to know.

He'd chosen to go to the door...

She was dead anyway. There was no time.

"Door blocked!" she screamed.

But she had no time for anything further.

The giant shoved her face in the sink now. She tried to thrash, to twist. He slapped her again—her skull was ringing.

She heard a loud *thump*. And realized the giant had shut the bathroom door and locked it. Then, muttering, he released her briefly. She watched in horror as he *pulled* the toilet out of the ground. His muscles strained like bowling balls. Exhausted, she slumped against the sink, trying to move towards the door. But he shoved her back. Then used the toilet as a wedge against the door.

She managed a brief glimpse of her phone, useless, reflecting the light above the sink.

But now the bedroom door was blocked. The bathroom door was blocked.

No windows in the bathroom.

She was dead.

She knew it.

Artemis had often wondered how she'd die. She'd often thought her father would do it. She still didn't know if Otto had a hand in all this. She was beginning to think not.

Though it didn't really matter.

The big man, now that he'd blocked the door, was breathing heavily. He grabbed her by the throat and began to squeeze again.

"Three minutes, smartass," he roared at her, spittle flecking her face. He seemed to have given up on the sink or the tub.

Now, he was choking her to death, pressing her spine against the cold, hard surface of the sink.

Nothing she could do. Nothing to say. She tried weakly to kick, but her feet ricocheted off pure muscle.

Forester was no longer shouting. The blows against the barricaded door had stopped. There was no use. He'd never make it in time. If he tried to reach the window... she didn't have any longer.

Dark spots gave way to sheer blindness.

She couldn't breathe, but she was so battered, disoriented, that this didn't even hurt.

She occasionally glimpsed flashes of shadow where the big man stared down at her, his face twisted into a horrible snarl.

Clap. Clap.

A pause. His grip lessened. And then she fell completely, landing on a floor flooded from the tub, the sink and the demolished toilet.

Her vision came back, slowly, but she had enough time to glimpse the giant murderer. He was still standing over her, blinking in confusion and staring at his image in the mirror.

Two red dots had appeared on his forehead. The mirror on the door suggested those holes had *entered* through the *back* of his head...

Artemis stared, trying to make sense of it.

And then the giant toppled. She didn't even have the energy to move as he landed on top of her, pinning her to the floor.

She grunted, straining under an armpit, trying to push him aside. As she did, she noted rivulets of red now streaming, swirling, moving with the water *under* the door to the hotel bathroom.

She sat in five inches of water, gasping, covered in the killer's blood, and utterly confused.

The panic, the fear, slowly dissipated to sheer relief.

But how had...

And then she spotted it.

Two bullet holes in the drywall of the flimsy hotel room wall, just above the phone she'd placed. She heard more shouting. Then an eye appeared in one of the holes. A dark, stubborn eye. A muted voice, muffled by drywall. "Artemis? Are you okay!"

She gasped again, spitting water, and trying to shove the giant off her before he pushed her under the liquid. "H-help," she tried louder. "Door... door blocked. Window!"

"Got it!" Forester yelled. He was already moving. The eye left the hole in the wall. She heard rapid, pounding footsteps, sprinting back down the hall, then to the stairs.

She just stared at the two holes in the wall.

Forester had used the video feed with her call to track the killer in the bathroom. The killer had been watching them, using an eye in the sky...

She supposed they'd simply returned the favor.

Soaked, covered in blood, her throat as sore as anything, she tried her best to keep her mouth above water, even as four hundred pounds of muscle and ill intent crushed down on her.

23

Artemis sat in the small-town hospital bed. She could see Agent Wade through her window. He was sitting on the bench outside the door. Forester had been keeping guard before, but after she'd gone to sleep, he'd vanished. Artemis guessed that Grant had forced him to get some rest.

The small hospital didn't *usually* require a personal security team.

But given some of her run-ins with the Dawkins family, Grant had decided it was justified.

Artemis shifted in the small cot, her head on the pillow. She had to give Grant her due. The woman knew how to take care of her agents and consultants. Artemis wasn't sure how things would have been if she *hadn't* helped solve the case.

But now...

A personal security guard.

It felt nice.

Though after what had happened the previous night, she wasn't sure she'd ever feel secure again.

Which was why she'd reached the conclusion she had…

Artemis swallowed, wincing at the bandages on her throat. Mostly, her neck was bruised, but the bandages were for some of the nastier scrapes left by the killer's fingernails. She also had a gash along her side from where she'd slipped along the sink.

But otherwise, Artemis was in good spirits.

That was, until Agent Grant pushed through the door.

The woman appeared like a ghost, her white hair shifting on the other side of the glass. Her perfectly manicured fingers pushing the door open.

The woman paused; glanced over her shoulder; held up a hand, indicating someone Artemis couldn't see; then stepped into the hospital room.

Grant stared at her.

Artemis blinked back.

"Well," Grant said slowly. "You look better than I expected."

"Umm… Thank you."

Grant shook her head. "No... no, don't thank me. Not yet." The woman turned now, stiff and rigid as ever. She frowned out the window, across the street, but then turned back to Artemis, watching her.

Artemis watched back.

Grant didn't say a word.

Artemis wasn't in the mood for a staring contest. "Can I help you with something?" Speaking with her tender throat was still somewhat painful, so she did it slowly, with great caution.

"Yes... I'm supposed to mention your payment for consulting will be sent via check."

"Oh... All right. Thank you."

Grant didn't leave. She continued standing there, still watching Artemis.

"Umm. Something else?"

"Maybe," Grant said, sighing. "You..." she tapped her fingers together slowly. And for the first time, the woman seemed slightly nervous. The confidence, the poise, was temporarily gone. But she lifted her head, sniffed once, then pressed. "You helped. Thank you, Ms. Blythe."

"Oh... Well... that—that's nice." Artemis swallowed, wincing. "Umm... You're welcome."

Grant still didn't move.

Artemis was beginning to wonder if she was about to be assassinated in her hospital bed. It was a morbid thought, but Grant was acting so strangely.

"I... I also had a question," Grant said quietly.

"Oh?"

"Yes. I... what would you..." More tapping fingers. "What would you think about enrolling in a training course?"

"Wait... what type of training?"

"FBI field training." Grant said the sentence the same time as she sighed, carrying the words with her breath.

Artemis tried not to gape. "Are you joking?"

"No. I don't joke."

"No... I guess not. Well..." Artemis was stunned. She tried not to show it. She especially tried not to show that she'd been thinking about this back at the hotel. A fanciful consideration, really... Not serious...

But now?

She stared at Grant.

Artemis didn't like the idea of being trapped by anyone. The last two times she'd worked for Grant, she hadn't really had a choice.

She didn't want *anyone* to control her life.

But what if...

She sighed faintly and then shrugged. "Can I think about it?"

Grant nodded once. If anything, she almost seemed relieved, as if concerned she'd be laughed out of the room. "Yes. Of course. I can give you a week."

Artemis nodded. "That's fine."

Grant gave Artemis a final look. She said... "The FBI has resources. We're a team. We help each other... Do you understand?"

Artemis shook her head slowly.

Instead of clarifying, though, Grant just sighed, turned, adjusted her neat suit, and pushed back out of the door, strolling away.

Artemis sat upright, frowning, feeling the cushion of the small bed beneath her. She bit her lip, feeling a surge of unease.

Was it possible?

Did she dare even *consider* it?

The FBI?

She snorted at the thought, shaking her head.

What would her fans think? What would the chess community think?

Hell... what would her own *father* think.

This... if anything, would help her keep an eye on Otto. Keep tabs on what he was up to. He'd planted thoughts... put things in motion years ago. The postcards alone were something to worry about.

Her father was making moves, and she still didn't know *why*.

How had her father known about Forester's past? How had her father known any of it?

She sighed in frustration.

But there were downsides too.

The FBI?

For one, she hated suits. But also… her run-ins with the police, especially in her youth, hadn't given her a very favorable view of law enforcement. Plus, there was the whole business with her relation t o—

Tap. Tap. Tap.

She frowned, glancing around.

Tap. Tap.

She turned and then glared. Her brother was by the third-floor window of the small hospital, waving urgently at her and nodding towards the latch.

She looked away. Grant had already disappeared down the hall.

Taptaptap. Louder and faster.

She huffed but then winced at the pain caused by the sound. She reached up, tenderly massaging her neck. Then, with a resigned sigh—a slower breath of air this time—she reached out and brushed the curtains around her bed aside. She stared towards the window as she slowly, with wobbly motions, got out of her bed.

The hospital gown was a modest one, thank goodness. But she still felt very uncomfortable walking towards the window.

She'd especially felt uncomfortable when Forester had been the one watching her hospital room. Wearing only her underwear beneath the thin fabric while Forester had kept an eye on her had nearly given her a panic attack.

Now, she reached the window, opened it, but placed a hand out, preventing Tommy from climbing through.

"No!" she said.

Tommy's head bounced off her hand, and he nearly fell. He cursed, latching one arm through the window and holding on. "Dammit... Are you trying to kill me?"

"Why can't you just use a door like normal people?"

He glared at her. "Not allowed back here."

"Why not?" she said, eyes narrowed.

He shrugged, though he caught the motion so he wouldn't fall. He was balanced on a drainpipe by the looks of things. But as she peered past him, towards the garden bed below, she said, "Looks like those bushes could break your fall. Good luck, Tommy."

"Fine—fine! I... I may have borrowed some pills last time I was here." He licked his lips nervously, his long hair framing his sharp features.

She sighed. "Borrowed pills?"

"Yeah... yeah, shit. Look, can I come in?"

"What do you want?"

"I heard you were nearly killed."

"I'm fine."

"What's wrong with your neck?"

"I'm fine, Tommy. I don't have the time for this." She'd meant to say *you* but changed the final word at the last moment.

He frowned at her. "Fine... whatever, Art. Be that way. I was just trying to be nice." He shrugged again and began to clamber down the pipe now.

She stared as his head disappeared from view, his long hair swishing past the sill. She wanted to just let him leave. To sulk off into a corner somewhere. She refused to be emotionally manipulated. Then again ...

What if he really was just concerned about her? But stealing pills? She almost pushed him off the ledge into the shrubs herself.

But then, she said, "Thank you."

He looked up. She peered out of the window, glaring at her brother. A couple of pedestrians across the street were watching in amusement, licking at ice cream cones they'd bought from the corner shop.

Tommy nodded once.

She hesitated... frowned, sighed, then said, "One thing... real quick..."

He looked up at her again, raising an eyebrow. The two neck tattoos shifted as he swallowed nervously.

"I... would you hate me if... if I started training to... Just to check it out. No real commitment. Just to... try..."

"Try what?" he said, gripping the pipe and using a second-floor windowsill for footing.

"Could you just... be careful."

"I'm fine. Try what?"

"The FBI has an opportunity for training. Agent Grant said—"

"Who's Agent Grant?"

"Not important. But what do you think—"

He shrugged at her. "Don't care. Go for it. Didn't even know you were alive until last week, sis."

She frowned. "You said you knew I was still playing chess."

"Hyperbole," he muttered, adjusting his grip with his fingerless gloves. Artemis heard a faint sound behind her, and she glanced back to see a nurse frowning, slowly approaching.

"Ma'am?" The nurse said. "Is everything okay?"

Artemis nodded primly. "My brother is climbing your building. Apologies. One moment." She turned back, frowning at Tommy. "So, you wouldn't be mad?"

"You care what I think?" he said. "Who are you talking to by the way."

"Nurse, in here," Artemis replied. "Ah—yes, there she goes. I think she's fetching security, Tommy."

He shook his head. "Dammit. Look, Art, just... If you see any orange bottles in there with a label that reads —"

"Not a chance!" she snapped.

Tommy rolled his eyes, but slid down the pipe the rest of the way and hopped off into the garden. The doors below opened, and two men in blue uniforms emerged, scowling and shouting after her brother. He hastened away, clambering like a monkey up a low wall and disappearing behind a parking structure.

A second later, she heard the loud grumble of a motorcycle engine.

She couldn't see it, but she didn't doubt Tommy had found a new bike.

He'd blown up his last one with plastic explosives.

She shook her head, muttering darkly, wincing and slowly closing the window. She took a moment to catch her breath, leaning back against the glass.

She still didn't know if her father had been involved with all of this. Didn't know how the postcards factored in. She was determined to find out though. If her father was up to something in Pinelake, she wanted to do everything she could to stop him.

But also...

She frowned, head pressed against the cold glass. She glanced towards where Agent Wade was working on a crossword puzzle, a pair of reading glasses on his nose. People were full of surprises.

FBI training... Grant's suggestion had made her uncomfortable...

But as she thought about it...

The giant had manhandled her. She hadn't even had a chance.

But stopping him? Stopping Mr. Kramer? Putting men like her father behind bars?

What if *that* was what she was meant to do?

She would still train for next month's tournament.

Of course she would.

She felt light-headed all of a sudden and stumbled back towards her bed, hearing the sound of her doctor's voice yelling at the nurse. Footsteps hastened down the hall outside her room.

Feeling much like Tommy, she slipped onto her bed quickly, throwing the covers back in place and closing her eyes, pretending to sleep.

It wasn't like she would have to stay in Pinelake. She could help the FBI—occasionally—anywhere...

Agent Forester didn't factor in at all. Neither did Grant... No... At least... mostly no.

But Helen Blythe... Artemis' sister...

She still didn't know if her father was lying. Didn't know what Otto Blythe was up to in Pinelake. But if there was even half a chance her sister was alive... Artemis was determined to find out.

And if possible... rescue Helen from whatever hellhole she'd been trapped in for the last seventeen years.

The door swished open. The doctor and nurse came hastily in. Artemis closed her eyes completely, head pressed to a pillow, feigning sleep.

But her mind was alert, spinning, whirring. Strategizing and considering all the possibilities ahead.

Would she take Grant up on her offer?

Maybe... maybe though, there was another way...

She couldn't be sure. Not yet. She'd have to think about it some more. Grant had said she had a week to consider the offer...

A lot could happen in a week.

The End

Chessmaster and FBI consultant, Artemis Blythe, will have to keep her wits about her as she visits her old man, the Ghostkiller, in prison.

A Notorious murdered who targeted seven women in the sleepy town of Pinelake.

Artemis only wants one thing: to discover if her sister, Helen, is still alive.

But her father is making moves of his own. And now, outside the walls of the prison, a giant of a killer is drowning the daughters of powerful men ...

Artemis pits her wits against her father, the new killer, and anyone else in town who scorns her family name.

Once a hypnotist with her own TV show, now, Sophie Quinn works as a full-time consultant for the FBI. Everything changed six years ago. She can still remember that horrible night. Slated to be the River Killer's tenth victim, she managed to slip her bindings and barely escape where so many others failed. Her sister wasn't so lucky.

And now the killer is back.

Two PHDs later, she's now a rising star at the FBI. Her photographic memory helps solve crimes, but also helps her to *never* forget. She saw the River Killer's tattoo. She knows what he sounds like. And now, ten years later, he's active again.

Sophie Quinn heads back home to the swamps of Louisiana, along the Mississippi River, intent on evening the score and finding the man who killed her sister. It's been six years since she's been home, though. Broken relationships and shattered dreams exist among the bayous, the rivers, the waterways and swamps of Louisiana; can Sophie find her way home again? Or will she be the River Killer's next victim to float downstream?

new assignment? She allowed a prolific serial killer to escape custody.

But what no one knows is that she did it on purpose.

The day she shows up in Nome, bags still unpacked, the wife of the richest gold miner in town goes missing. This is the second woman to vanish in as many days. And it's up to Ella to find out what happened.

Assigning Ella to Nome is no accident, either. Though she swore she'd never return, Ella grew up in the small, gold mining town, treated like royalty as a child due to her own family's wealth. But like all gold tycoons, the Porter family secrets are as dark as Ella's own.

WANT TO KNOW MORE?

GREENFIELD PRESS IS THE brainchild of bestselling author Steve Higgs. He specializes in writing fast paced adventurous mystery and urban fantasy with a humorous lilt. Having made his money publishing his own work, Steve went looking for a few 'special' authors whose work he believed in.

Georgia Wagner was the first of those, but to find out more and to be the first to hear about new releases and what is coming next, you can join the Facebook group by clicking the link below. Or copying the following link into your browser - www.facebook.com/GreenfieldP ress.

About the Author

Georgia Wagner

Georgia Wagner worked as a ghost writer for many, many years before finally taking the plunge into self-publishing. Location and character are two big factors for Georgia, and getting those right allows the story to flow seamlessly onto the page. And flow it does, because Georgia is so prolific a new term is required to describe the rate at which nerve-tingling stories find their way into print.

When not found attached to a laptop, Georgia likes spending time in local arboretums, among the trees and ponds. An avid cultivator of orchids, begonias, and all things floral, Georgia also has a strong penchant for art, paintings, and sculptures. A many-decades long passion for mystery novels and years of chess tournament experience makes Georgia the perfect person to pen the Artemis Blythe series.